Why him?

Was it his movie-star looks? His charm? His intelligence? Or was it the power of his desire that was seducing and compelling her? Men had wanted her before but never quite like this.

This was something else.

Her cheeks continued to burn as her eyes met his, her heart rate not yet calmed. If she felt like this after one kiss, then how would she feel once she was in bed with him, their bodies naked, and his flesh inside of hers?

A quiver rippled down her spine.

Legally wed,
But he's never said...
"I love you."

They're...

The series where marriages are
made in haste...and love comes later....

Look out for more WEDLOCKED! wedding
stories available only from Harlequin Presents®

Coming next month:
The Billion-Dollar Bride
by Kay Thorpe
#2462

Coming in May:
The Disobedient Bride
by Helen Bianchin
#2463

Coming in June:
The Moretti Marriage
by Catherine Spencer
#2474

Miranda Lee

HIS BRIDE FOR ONE NIGHT

Wedlocked!

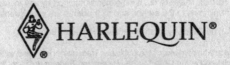

HARLEQUIN®

TORONTO • NEW YORK • LONDON
AMSTERDAM • PARIS • SYDNEY • HAMBURG
STOCKHOLM • ATHENS • TOKYO • MILAN • MADRID
PRAGUE • WARSAW • BUDAPEST • AUCKLAND

ISBN 0-373-12451-1

HIS BRIDE FOR ONE NIGHT

First North American Publication 2005.

Copyright © 2005 by Miranda Lee.

This edition published by arrangement with Harlequin Books S.A.

® and TM are trademarks of the publisher. Trademarks indicated with ® are registered in the United States Patent and Trademark Office, the Canadian Trade Marks Office and in other countries.

www.eHarlequin.com

Printed in U.S.A.

CHAPTER ONE

DANIEL stared down through the plane window at the panoramic beauty of the city and coastline below. The captain had just announced a slight delay in landing at Mascot Airport and was doing a sweeping circle over Sydney to give his mainly tourist passengers a good look at the city which reputedly had the best harbour—and the best beaches—in the world.

Not an exaggerated claim, in Daniel's opinion. He'd flown over some pretty spectacular cities in his time. New York. San Francisco. Rio.

But Sydney was in a class of its own.

Maybe it was the early-morning light which made its beaches look whiter than white, and the water bluer than blue. But just the sight of that dazzling harbour with its famous icons of the bridge and the opera house—each one sparkling in the summer sunshine—lightened Daniel's spirits.

Beth had been right to insist he come home, even if only for a visit.

Home…

Funny how he always thought of Sydney as home. True, he'd been born here. And yes, he'd gone to school here from the age of twelve to eighteen, which was why he didn't have much of an American accent. But most of his life had been spent in the States. In

Los Angeles, to be precise. The city of angels. Or devils, depending on your point of view.

LA could be one tough city. Usually, Daniel could handle its toughness. One could say he'd thrived on it.

But life had finally got the better of him. This last Christmas had been particularly bleak and lonely, with his mother having died earlier that year.

A shudder rippled down Daniel's spine. It was eight months since his poor mom had passed away, but it felt like yesterday.

He still didn't know how he'd controlled himself when his father showed up at her funeral with his new wife on his arm. His fourth. Blonde, of course. And young. They were always blonde and young. And his father was what now? Sixty-five, ten years older than his mother would have been next month. Still, successful producers never seemed to have trouble attracting—and marrying—ambitious young starlets.

His own mother had had stars in her eyes when she'd first met the handsome Ben Bannister on a star-finding trip to Sydney. He'd been a very experienced thirty whereas she was a naive twenty.

Daniel often wondered why his father had married his mother. The pretty little brunette from Bondi didn't seem his style. OK, so he'd got her pregnant, but was that reason enough to marry? Far better that he'd gone back to America and left her to raise her son by herself here in Australia.

None of his father's marriages lasted very long. A few years at the most. But they always produced a child or two. Daniel had several half-brothers and -sisters whom he barely knew. His father no longer lived in Los Angeles, having moved to New York after he left Daniel's mother when Daniel was six. Or had he been seven?

Must have been seven, Daniel mused. He was six years older than his little sister, Beth, who'd just begun to walk at the time.

Whatever, he'd been old enough to be almost as hurt as his mother, his sweet, soft-hearted mother, who had never got over her husband's betrayal. Before his father stormed out of the front door, he'd callously told his weeping wife that he'd been unfaithful to her all along. She'd turned to pills for comfort at first. Then drink. And finally other men, younger men who used her body and spent her settlement money like water.

When things became really bad, Daniel's maternal grandfather stepped in and took Beth and himself back to Australia to live with him, making sure they got a good education and a more stable upbringing. Both children loved life in Sydney with their widower grandfather, Beth especially. Within months, she was saying she wanted to stay forever. Daniel liked the life too, but he was older and couldn't help worrying about his mother. She sounded OK in her letters, claimed she'd stopped drinking and had a job, but she always had some excuse why she couldn't fly out and visit.

Once he'd completed high school, Daniel felt compelled to return to Los Angeles, where he'd been relieved to see that his mom *had* stopped drinking, but oh…how she'd aged. Yes, she did have a job, but it didn't pay much and she was living in a dump. Unable to convince her to return to Australia with him—a warped form of pride, in his opinion—Daniel borrowed some money from his grandfather, found somewhere better for them both to live, then enrolled at a local university to study law. He worked three part-time jobs to pay his fees, and to make sure his mother wanted for nothing.

When he graduated top of his class, the prestigious LA law firm of Johansen, O'Neill and Morecroft snapped Daniel up and he soon found his feet as their most aggressive and successful divorce lawyer. Soon he was able to repay his grandfather every cent he'd borrowed, plus interest. When his impressive first-year bonus came in he put down a deposit on a maintenance-free condominium for his mother, and a nearby bachelor pad for himself. As much as he adored his mother, Daniel felt it was high time he had his own space.

In the first few years of his career as a divorce lawyer, Daniel represented both men and women, but when he made partner shortly after his thirtieth birthday he announced that in future the only clients he would represent were women. The men he left to someone else.

Daniel found great satisfaction in preventing sleazebag husbands with more money than morals from weaseling their way out of paying what was due to their ex-wives. He was ruthless in his quest to gain financial security for the discarded, disillusioned and distressed women who trailed through his office. Women who were no longer young enough, or pretty enough, or exciting enough for the husbands who'd once promised to love, honour and cherish them forever.

Daniel was particularly vicious in his pursuit of justice if there were children involved, especially when the men in question didn't want to face their responsibility regarding hands-on child-rearing. And there were plenty of those.

Men who abandoned their children had to be made to pay.

'But not all men are like that,' his more optimistic little sister had recently said to him over the phone during her weekly call from Sydney. Beth never had returned to America, even after her beloved grandfather passed away. 'If my marriage ever broke up, Vince would never abandon our child. Or children. I'm not sure how many we'll have. But more than one.'

Beth was currently seven months pregnant with her first child.

'Not that our marriage is ever going to break up,' Beth had added quickly. 'We have our ups and downs but we're still very much in love with each other.'

In love, Daniel mused as the jumbo jet banked and began its descent into Sydney.

What was being *in love*, exactly?

He'd never felt it, he was sure. Not once. Thirty-six years old, and he'd never fallen in love.

He'd liked lots of women. And lusted after them. And made love to them.

But that wasn't the same as being in love. He'd never been so overcome by mad passion that he'd do anything for the object of said passion, such as ask her to marry him. Even if he did fall in love one day, Daniel couldn't see himself marrying. He'd seen far too many divorces!

'You're a cynical, cold-blooded bastard,' his last ladyfriend had flung at him just before she'd flounced out of his office—and his life—a couple of weeks before Christmas. 'I refuse to waste any more time on you, Daniel Bannister. You obviously don't love me. I doubt you even know what love is.'

All true, he'd finally agreed after she'd stormed out, her fury forcing him to have a long, hard look at himself.

What he'd discovered had been sobering.

He'd always condemned his father for being a serial husband, but he wasn't much better when it came to relationships. He'd become a serial lover, going from one woman to another, never committing himself, never losing much sleep when these relationships—such as they were—were terminated.

Yep. He was a cynical, cold-blooded bastard all right. Not quite the noble, knight-in-shining-armour type he'd always imagined himself to be.

Two months later he was in a plane circling Sydney, still trying to come to terms with this revised character assessment of himself, trying to justify his past behaviour. Not very successfully. OK, so he hadn't ever lied to his ladyfriends, or promised anything serious, or betrayed any vows, or abandoned any children. But he'd still hurt the women he'd dated, and who had probably wanted more from him than what he'd been prepared to give.

Daniel understood that he was a good catch, as the saying went. Physically attractive, professionally successful, financially secure. The kind of guy that his married acquaintances were always trying to set up with their single, female, husband-hunting friends.

To give himself some credit, Daniel always steered clear of the more obvious traps, sticking to women whom he'd mistakenly believed were dedicated career girls.

Only in hindsight did he realise that thirty-something girls who'd devoted their lives to their careers often had a change of heart when their biological clocks started ticking. Suddenly, some of them began to want wedding bells and baby bootees, whereas in the beginning all they'd wanted was some stimulating conversation over dinner and some satisfying sex at the end of the night.

Which he was more than happy to provide.

As Daniel stared through the plane window, his eyes glazed over and he started wondering if men ever suffered from the biological-clock syndrome. He'd turned thirty-six last month.

Maybe one day soon, he'd meet some girl and suddenly feel things he'd never felt before. Maybe he'd lose his head through love and desire and uncontrollable passion.

Daniel uttered a small, dry laugh.

Dream on, Daniel. This is *you* we're talking about here. That cynical, cold-blooded bastard. You'd be the last man on earth to lose his head over a woman!

The plane's wheels making contact with the tarmac startled Daniel. He'd been so wrapped up in his thoughts that he'd stopped following their descent.

His gaze focused again through the window to take in the view of Sydney from the ground.

A large bay of water stretched out before him on the plane's left, fringed by sand. Directly opposite was an industrial area. To his right, a residential suburb. Airports were usually on the outskirts of cities but Mascot wasn't far from Sydney's city centre.

His sister's house was in the eastern suburbs, at Rose Bay, also near the city centre. She'd promised to meet him, despite the early hour and her advanced pregnancy.

Daniel knew it would do him good to spend a couple of weeks here in Sydney with his sister and her husband. Australians were wonderfully easygoing, and Beth was Australian through and through now.

People blamed the hot weather, but Daniel didn't believe it had anything to do with the weather. He believed it had something to do with their isolation. They lived so far away that they hadn't yet been contaminated with the rest of the world's mad and bad habits. In his experience, Australians didn't seem to live to work as a lot of Americans did. They worked to live.

Daniel hoped to embrace some of that philosophy during his visit here. He was in danger of becoming a serious workaholic.

All work and no play made Daniel a very dull boy.

A fortnight of total relaxation would do him a power of good.

CHAPTER TWO

CHARLOTTE responded to the annoying beep-beep of her clock alarm as any person would at five a.m. on a Friday morning, especially one who'd only got to bed at two. She flung an arm over her duvet, cut the irritating noise off by hitting the snooze button, then rolled over and curled up again for ten more minutes' precious sleep.

But before she could return to the bliss of oblivion, Charlotte suddenly remembered why she'd set her alarm at such a God-forsaken hour.

Gary's flight was due in at six-twenty.

Although it was not a long drive from Bondi to Mascot at that hour of the morning, Charlotte had known in advance that she'd need extra time to make herself look tippy-top to meet her fiancé. Hence her early alarm.

Throwing back the duvet, Charlotte leapt out of bed, swearing when she banged her leg on the corner of her bedside chest. Rubbing her thigh, she limped to the bathroom.

'Aaah!' she squawked when she finally saw herself in the mirror above the vanity.

Her screech of alarm was followed by the appearance of an equally dishevelled Louise in the bathroom door. 'What's all the noise about?' her flatmate asked blearily.

'Look at me!' Charlotte proclaimed with a despairing groan. 'This is all your fault, Louise. You should never have insisted on having my hen night only two days before my wedding, and the night before Gary's arrival. You know what even a few drinks do to me. Not to mention lack of sleep. My God, I look a positive fright!'

Louise snorted. 'You couldn't look a positive fright if your life depended on it. You even look good with dark roots.'

Charlotte groaned again. Louise had to be blind! Her hair was nothing short of appalling.

Maintaining herself as the long-haired, golden-locked blonde whom Gary had met and fallen instantly in love with up on the Gold Coast last year had taken its toll. All Charlotte and Louise's skills as hairdressers could not prevent the damage which had been done to her naturally thick, dark brown hair by continual bleaching.

She'd only gone blonde for that holiday in a fit of pique after her break-up with Dwayne. His new girlfriend was a blonde. Charlotte had never intended to keep it that way. She'd been planning on cutting it short afterwards and returning to her natural colour.

But her plans had changed on meeting Gary, and eight months later she was still a blonde. A blonde with dark roots and split ends.

Charlotte wished now she hadn't put off doing the roots till the day of her wedding. She should have had them done yesterday. And had a trim. *And* put in a treatment.

'I have to use the bathroom,' Louise said with a

yawn. 'Why don't you go make me some coffee, in exchange for which I'll blow-dry your hair for you?'

'Do you think you could give me a quick trim and an instant treatment as well?' Charlotte pleaded.

'What am I, your fairy godmother? OK, OK, just go get that coffee.'

One hour later Charlotte looked as good as she could, under the circumstances. But, truly, if she kept bleaching and blow-drying her hair so ruthlessly it would start breaking off, as Louise had pointed out.

'If Gary really loves you,' Louise had added drily, 'he wouldn't care if your hair's long or short. Or if you're a blonde or a brunette.'

Louise's words echoed in Charlotte's mind during the short drive to the airport.

If Gary really loves you…

It wasn't the first time Louise had expressed doubts over the reality of Gary's love for her. And vice versa.

Charlotte could understand her friend's misgivings. Most of her relationship with the good-looking American lawyer *had* developed over the internet, which was a trap in itself. Exchanging emails wasn't the same as actually spending time with each other. It was easy to put your best foot forward with words, rather than action. Charlotte did understand that.

But theirs hadn't been a strictly email romance. Their initial meeting had been in the flesh. Unfortunately, their time together had been brief. It had been the last night of her holiday on the Gold Coast. The last night of Gary's trip to Australia as well. He had been due to return to LA the next day.

Gary had spied her across a crowded room—actually, it was a smoke-filled club—and zeroed in on her straight away. He'd asked her to dance and the rest, as they say, was history.

They'd spent the whole night together. Not in bed or anything like that. Charlotte had never been the sort of girl to jump into bed at the drop of a hat, especially with some smooth-talking American out here on holiday. There was no doubt Gary wouldn't have minded, but he'd seemed impressed when she'd resisted his advances to have sex. Instead, they'd walked along the beach for hours, hand in hand, just talking. As they'd watched the sun come up together, he told her she was the girl he'd waited for all his life.

Later that day she'd accompanied Gary to the airport, where he'd promised to call her as soon as he got home. His passionate goodbye kiss had sent her head spinning, repairing some of the damage Dwayne had perpetrated on her battered self-esteem.

Louise had warned her when she came back to Sydney that men met on holiday rarely contacted you afterwards. But Gary had. He'd called Charlotte as soon as he'd returned to Los Angeles and they'd been in constant contact ever since, sometimes by phone, but mostly by email.

Charlotte felt she knew Gary much better than she'd even known Dwayne, the rat on whom she'd wasted the previous two years of her life. He'd eventually dumped her for some gym bunny, whom he'd got pregnant.

When Gary asked her to marry him last November, Charlotte hadn't hesitated to say yes.

Maybe she would have hesitated if he hadn't been prepared to marry her here in Sydney, and make his life here.

Or if you weren't thirty-three, another nasty little voice whispered in her head. *And beginning to believe that you would never find a husband.*

Charlotte swiftly brushed that no longer relevant thought aside.

She *was* getting married. Tomorrow. And in considerable style.

Charlotte hoped Gary wouldn't mind. He'd requested a simple wedding. No church. Just a celebrant, and only a small guest list. He himself had no close family; his parents had been killed in a tragic house fire when he was a teenager.

But Charlotte's father hadn't waited thirty-three years to give his youngest daughter away in anything less than a white wedding with all the trimmings.

Secretly, Charlotte had been glad her father had insisted on this. Her two older sisters had both been beautiful brides with white wedding gowns, and Charlotte hadn't really wanted to settle for anything less. The church part she'd managed to skirt around, her parents reluctantly agreeing to a celebrant. But everything else was to be very traditional, complete with a proper reception, a three-tiered wedding cake, the bridal waltz. The lot!

Charlotte hadn't informed Gary of any of this. She reasoned that once he was here, she could explain that it wasn't her doing. It was her parents' idea. And it wasn't as though he had to pay for any of it. Her father had footed the bill, dear sweet man that he was. All Gary had to do was be fitted with a rental tux today—a fitting had been arranged for this afternoon—then show up in it tomorrow.

Charlotte didn't think that was too much to ask. Not of a man who really loved her. And he did. He must really love her, otherwise he wouldn't be coming all this way to marry her. Or have sent her such a lovely sapphire and diamond engagement ring.

Just the sight of it on her ring finger was reassuring.

Half an hour later, Charlotte was pacing back and forth outside the arrivals gate to which Gary's flight had been allotted, her eyes darting continuously to the ramp down which her fiancé would walk any moment now. His plane had only touched down ten minutes earlier—it had been late landing—but business class passengers were rarely held up in Customs.

She couldn't stand still. Nerves had her stomach in knots. But was she excited or afraid, afraid that she was about to rush into marriage with a man she hadn't even been to bed with?

Still, maybe that was a good thing. She'd eventually slept with most of her other boyfriends and none of them had proposed marriage. Perhaps because she'd always ultimately disappointed them, sexually. Her lack of enjoyment seemed to bother her boyfriends more than it did her.

She'd been totally honest with Gary and he'd reassured her he wasn't marrying her because she was a sexpot, but because she was beautiful and warm and sweet and wanted what he wanted. A family. At the same time, he seemed extremely confident that everything would turn out fine on their wedding night.

Charlotte hoped so, hoped that this time she would feel the earth move the way Louise was always talking about.

If she didn't? Well...as Gary said, they would work on it together.

There! There he was!

She started jumping up and down, waving and smiling.

'Here! Here! Over here!'

When he turned his darkly handsome head from where he'd been looking over to one side, Charlotte's hand froze mid-air, her smile instantly fading.

Because it wasn't Gary at all. Just someone who looked like him. In broad strokes, that was. About the same height. Gary was over six feet. Similar hair. Dark brown. Short. No parting. Rather similar in profile as well. High forehead, strong nose, square jaw.

But when this man stared straight at her, Charlotte could see his eyes were nothing like Gary's. This man's were deeper set, and very penetrating. Not blue, either, but brown. Almost black when they narrowed underneath his dark straight brows.

They were narrowed right now. On her.

Never in her life had Charlotte been looked at the way this man was looking at her. The focused intensity in his gaze was nothing short of blistering.

When he started pushing his luggage trolley towards her, Charlotte's arm dropped back down to

clutch her shoulder bag across her chest in a
strangely defensive fashion. Despite her stomach
curling with embarrassment, she found she could not
look away from him, but kept on staring back into
those darkly magnetic eyes.

'Did Beth send you to meet me?' he asked as he
ground to a halt in front of her, his accent not dis-
similar to Gary's.

Dear God, *Gary*! In her fluster, she'd forgotten all
about him.

'I'm sorry, no,' she apologised swiftly, dragging
her eyes away from the disturbing stranger to see if
Gary had made an appearance. 'I don't know anyone
named Beth. I…I thought you were my fiancé for a
moment,' she rattled on, her eyes agitatedly searching the now constant line of exiting passengers.

But Gary wasn't amongst them.

She glanced back at the American, who was still
standing there. He was still staring at her as well, but
now with an air of curiosity, whereas before his eyes
had carried…what, exactly?

She wasn't sure.

'You…um…look like him. Sort of.' In truth, Gary
was not quite in this man's league. Gary was good-
looking. This man was heart-thumpingly handsome.

'Aah,' he said. 'I see.'

The obvious disappointment in his voice and eyes
rattled Charlotte. What had he been thinking? Or
hoping?

'We're getting married tomorrow,' she added, for
goodness knew what reason. She'd already explained
why she'd waved and smiled at him.

'Lucky man,' he murmured, his gaze moving slowly over her from head to toe.

Suddenly she knew what she'd seen in his eyes earlier, and why he'd sounded disappointed just now.

Charlotte had encountered desire in lots of men before, but never had the message been delivered with such high voltage, and by such incredible eyes. They weren't just beautiful, but intelligent and intriguing, and very sexy.

Her feminine antennae quivered as his message was received once more, the current charging through her veins heating her body from the inside out.

Charlotte could not have been more shocked when her face actually flamed. Why, she hadn't blushed in years!

'If you'll excuse me,' she said, and forced her legs to carry her away from his disturbing presence. But even as she went back to searching for Gary, her mind still lingered on the handsome stranger. Who was he? *What* was he? And what was he doing here in Sydney?

CHAPTER THREE

DANIEL was almost grateful when she gave him the brush-off. What on earth had he been doing, staring at her like that?

Hitting on women had never been his style. On top of that, she was a blonde. One of the bottled variety. Daniel had an aversion to bottled blondes.

To be fair to himself, she wasn't the usual bottle blonde, the kind his father married. The kind Daniel often met in LA, the ones whose over-bleached, over-teased hair was not the only thing false about them.

Despite the dark roots, this girl's hair was sleek and simply styled, falling in a straight curtain halfway down her back. There was nothing even remotely false about her face, either, which was as beautiful as it was refreshingly natural. If she was wearing make-up, it had been applied with a light hand. Her skin didn't need enhancement, anyway, being fine and clear and olive-toned. Her eyes were just as naturally beautiful. Big and blue as the Pacific, with the longest, darkest lashes.

She did have lip gloss on. Her lips had definitely looked extra shiny when he'd stared at them. Shiny and wet and full. The kind of lips made for kissing, and for being kissed by, and for...

Daniel pulled himself up sharply and whirled away

22

from where he'd been standing, still staring after her. It had been a long time since he'd been knocked for six by a woman at first sight. And an even longer time since he had no chance at all in being successful with one he fancied as much as he'd instantly fancied this one.

An intelligent man had to know when a female target was worth pursuing, and when she was not. This girl was getting married tomorrow. He couldn't expect her to fall at his feet. Couldn't expect her to respond to him in any way.

Which perhaps was what was still bothering him. Because she *had* responded to him, hadn't she? He'd seen the flash of sexual connection in her eyes. He'd spotted the telling tension in her body language. Sensed that she'd been as startled by her attraction to him as he'd been by his for her.

The way she'd blushed when he'd looked her up and down might have been embarrassment. But he suspected not. She was a woman, not some naive young girl.

No, she'd responded to him all right, which was a source of great irritation.

Daniel was not a man who liked to lose at anything in life. But this time, he had to accept defeat gracefully. Had to ignore the signs of mutual attraction and move on. Literally.

With a sigh, he started searching the crowded arrivals area for his sister, deliberately making sure he didn't go back the way the blonde had gone. The last thing he wanted was to see her throwing her arms around some other man. His male ego was still smarting. His male body wasn't feeling crash hot, either.

But Beth was nowhere to be found. Yet she should have been here. The plane had been late enough landing.

If Beth had one flaw it was chronic tardiness.

The beeping of his cellphone had Daniel pulling it out and putting it to his ear.

'Yes, Beth,' he said drily.

'I'm sorry, Daniel, but I overslept. I was so excited to see you today that I couldn't sleep at first last night. So I lay down on the sofa to watch TV and I must have drifted off there. So I wasn't in my bed to hear the alarm and Vince, of course, would have just banged the button down and gone back to sleep.'

'Fine. I'll catch a taxi.'

'No, no, don't do that. I *am* on my way. Have some breakfast in the coffee shop down the far end of Arrivals and I'll be there in around twenty minutes, OK?'

'OK,' he agreed, resignation in his voice.

'You're not mad at me?'

'No.'

'I'm amazed!'

'I decided on the plane to be more relaxed in future,' he informed her with a somewhat ironic smile. Relaxed was not how he was feeling at this moment. Clearly, he needed more practice at being laid-back. And in handling sexual frustration.

'No kidding. That'll be a first. Look, I have to hang up. I can't risk being booked talking on my mobile whilst driving. I've already lost three points on my licence for speeding. See you soon. Bye.'

'Bye,' Daniel replied into an already dead phone.

Smiling wryly to himself, he slipped the phone into his pocket, then pushed his luggage trolley down to the coffee shop Beth had directed him to. Once he'd ordered a mug of flat white at the counter—he'd had breakfast on the plane—he settled himself at a clean table, stretched his legs out, crossed his arms and started surveying the world passing by.

Bad idea.

For who should be coming towards him but the gorgeous blonde, *without* a fiancé by her side? She was walking very slowly, with a cute little pink cellphone clamped to her ear, totally unaware of him, her lovely head down, her concentration on the conversation she was having.

Once again, Daniel could not take his eyes off her. Not her face so much this time, but her body, which in slow motion was a sight to behold. His first visual port of call were her breasts—especially in that tight pink top. Full and lush, with perky nipples which even the confines of a bra could not hide. There was nothing wrong with her lower half, either. Small waist. Womanly hips. Flat stomach. Long legs. Slender ankles.

Daniel liked shapely girls in tight jeans, especially hipster jeans that hugged their legs all the way down. He hated flares on a female. He liked to see their ankles. And their feet.

He noticed that she had pretty little feet, shown to advantage in open-toed, high-heeled sandals, her toenails painted the same candy-pink as her top. And her phone.

As she came closer he saw that she was looking pale. Pale and somewhat shaken. Clearly, she was receiving some bad news.

She ground to a halt within listening distance of Daniel's table. 'I don't believe it!' she cried out. 'Life couldn't be that cruel to me!'

Oh-oh. Something serious must have happened to her missing fiancé. As much as Daniel would like the blonde to be footloose and fancy-free, he wasn't selfish enough to hope her boyfriend had had an accident, or anything horrible like that.

'The bastard!' the blonde suddenly spat, and Daniel's eyebrows shot up.

Nope. Not an accident. The cad just hadn't shown up. By the sounds of things, he wasn't about to, either.

Despite his feeling sorry for the girl, all sorts of sexual vistas suddenly opened up before Daniel's eyes. When his conscience pricked, he ignored it. He was a normal, red-blooded male, after all, not a saint.

'No, I'll be all right,' the blonde said in clipped tones. 'No, I'm tougher than that. No, of course I'm not going to start crying. I'm in public, for pity's sake. I'll wait till I get home first. Or at least in the car.'

But she didn't wait till she got home. Or even in the car. No sooner had she said goodbye to whoever she was talking to than she burst into tears. Not quiet tears, either. Great, shoulder-racking sobs.

He could understand why the person on the other end of the phone had been worried about her crying.

Thanking fate, Daniel jumped to his feet and rushed to the rescue.

'Is there anything I can do to help?' he asked as he laid a firm, but gentle hand on one of her shaking shoulders.

Charlotte stiffened, then glanced up through her sodden lashes.

It was *him*, the handsome American she'd encountered earlier, the one she'd mistaken for Gary, the one who'd stared at her with hot, hungry eyes.

But they weren't hot, or hungry at the moment. They were looking at her with kindness and concern.

'Bad news, I gather.'

'You could say that,' Charlotte mumbled as she pulled a tissue out of her bag and dabbed at her nose.

'Look, why don't you come over and have some coffee with me?' the American invited, indicating a nearby table. 'I'm stuck here, waiting for my sister to arrive, and wouldn't mind a bit of company. Meanwhile, you can tell me why your fiancé didn't show up.'

Shock made her blink, then blink again. 'How on earth did you know that?'

'You told me yourself you'd mistaken me for your fiancé back at the exit gate,' he explained. 'There's no man by your side and you were just crying. It doesn't take much intelligence to put two and two together.'

'Oh. Yes, I see,' she said as she wiped her nose again, then took a deep, gathering breath.

'So, have you been temporarily stood up?' he asked. 'Or fully jilted?'

'Fully jilted, I'm afraid,' she said dully, her earlier distress gradually being replaced by despair. How *could* fate be so cruel? And what on earth was she going to tell her parents?

'Some men are bloody fools,' the American said.

Charlotte might have been flattered, if she hadn't been feeling so devastated.

'Come on. A cup of coffee will do you the world of good.'

Charlotte was beyond protesting when he took her elbow and led her over to the table. The many-times-bitten part of her knew the American probably had his own agenda in being nice to her. But she wasn't too worried. They were in public. She was quite safe. If he wanted to buy her a cup of coffee, then he could. She was in no fit state to drive home just yet, anyway.

But she had no intention of telling him a single personal detail. He was a perfect stranger, for heaven's sake!

The next couple of minutes passed in a blank blur. Charlotte just sat there in a daze whilst the American ordered her a cappuccino. When it arrived soon after his own mug of coffee, he heaped in a couple of spoonfuls of sugar and pushed it over in front of her.

'Drink up,' he advised. 'You need a sugar hit. You're in shock.'

She did, and soon began to feel marginally better.

'Thank you,' she said at last. 'You were right. I needed that.'

'Aren't you going to tell me what happened?'

'Why on earth would you be interested?' she countered, just a tad stroppily. Charlotte knew he didn't really give a damn about her personal pain. He was just trying to pick her up.

His knight-to-the-rescue act. The coffee. His seemingly kind questions. All weapons to get what he wanted. *Her*.

She'd met his kind before. Overseas visitors who were always on the look-out for female company whilst they were away. He probably had a wife at home, or a live-in lover, or at least a girlfriend. Men who looked and dressed like him were rarely unattached. That suit he was wearing was not of the off-the-peg variety. His gold watch looked expensive as well, as did his gold and diamond dress ring.

He smiled, the gleam in his eyes carrying amusement and admiration. 'I see you're already on the road to recovery. That's good. You'll survive, then.'

'That depends on what you mean by survive,' she retorted. 'I have my parents driving down to Sydney today to meet my fiancé. Then the rest of my entire family will be arriving tomorrow to attend my wedding. Sisters. Aunts. Uncles. Nieces. Nephews. Cousins. All of them have been dying for me to get married for years. They're country, you see, and country people think marriage and motherhood is the only true career for a female. At last, I was going to be a success in their eyes...'

Tears threatened again, but she valiantly blinked them back.

'Tell me what happened with your fiancé,' he insisted.

She stared hard at him and wondered if she'd been wrong about his intentions. Those expressive eyes of his did seem genuinely sympathetic this time.

'Nothing much to tell,' she said with a weary shrug. 'He's not coming. The wedding's off. End of story.'

Again, she had to reach for a fresh tissue. Sympathy always set Charlotte off when she was upset.

He didn't press her to talk whilst she mopped her eyes once more, and this time she gathered herself more quickly. But as she sat there in wretched silence, having the occasional sip of coffee, Charlotte was suddenly filled with the urge to give vent to her feelings. What did it really matter if he was a stranger? she reasoned as anger started to simmer inside her. Probably better than his being a friend. Most of her friends were sick and tired of hearing about her relationship disasters.

'Louise was right,' she bit out, the coffee-cup clattering as she dropped it back into the saucer. 'He didn't really love me.'

'Who's Louise?'

'My best friend. We share a flat together.'

'She was the one on the phone to you just now, I presume.'

My, but he was a very observant man! And extremely intuitive.

She nodded her agreement. 'Apparently, Gary rang last night and left a message saying he wouldn't be on the plane and that he'd sent a long email, explaining everything, but we were out very late and didn't check the answering machine when we came in. Louise saw there was a message after I left this morning. She rang Gary to find out what was going on, but he didn't answer. I guess it's the middle of the night over there. So she rang me and I had her have a look at the email he sent.'

'That would be your missing fiancé's name? Gary?'

'Gary Cantrell. And he's not missing,' Charlotte ground out bitterly. 'He's in LA, with his *PA*. His *pregnant* PA, the one who somehow miraculously discovered she was having Gary's baby the same day he was supposed to be leaving to marry *me*!'

'Aah,' the American said knowingly.

'Yes. Aaah.'

'So how long has it been since you and Gary were together?'

'I haven't seen him since last June.'

'That's eight months ago!' His shocked tone carried a none too subtle message. Eight months was too long to leave any man on his own, in his opinion.

'I was faithful to *him*,' Charlotte snapped.

'That's commendable. But men are not renowned for their faithfulness when their fiancées—or wives—are a world away for such an extended period of time.'

'Tell me something new.'

'Why *were* you apart for so long?'

Charlotte sighed, then gave him a brief run-down on her romance with Gary, leaving out the fact she hadn't been to bed with him, but including her stupidly going against Gary's wishes and secretly planning a traditional wedding at a top Sydney hotel.

'I suppose you don't know the Regency Royale, being an American,' she said at this point.

'The name does ring a bell,' he replied.

'It's one of the plushest hotels in Sydney. Everything there is so expensive. I should be able to cancel the suite I booked for the wedding night, but the reception is a done deal. Know anyone who might want a three-tiered wedding cake and a designer wedding gown? Not to mention a five-day prepaid package holiday up at the Hunter Valley?'

Her father wasn't the only one who'd wasted a small fortune.

'Not at the moment. Maybe you can advertise them on the internet. You seem to be able to sell anything there.'

Charlotte groaned. 'Don't talk to me about the internet.'

'Just trying to be practical.'

'I know what you're thinking.'

'What am I thinking?'

'That internet romances are often little more than fantasies being played out by both parties. They're not real. Our love for each other wasn't real.'

'That is a widely held opinion,' he said.

'Maybe that was the case for Gary, but it wasn't for me. I loved him,' Charlotte cried. 'And I was going to marry him tomorrow.'

But even as she proclaimed the depth and sincerity of her love for Gary, Charlotte suspected there had been more than a touch of romantic fantasy about their whole relationship. A touch of desperation on her part as well.

Maybe it was all for the best that she wasn't marrying Gary.

But that didn't make her dismay or disappointment any easier to bear.

'Tomorrow is going to be the worst, most humiliating day of my life,' she declared, then grimaced. 'Actually no, *today* will probably take that prize. I'm supposed to be having lunch with my parents today, to introduce my fiancé in the flesh. I'd do anything in the world not to have to tell my father that the wedding's off. He's spent such a lot of money on this wedding, and he's not a rich man. Just a farmer. I'll pay him back, of course, but it will take me years on a hairdresser's pay.'

If only she hadn't treated herself to a new car last year, or that stupid honeymoon holiday. Her savings account was less than zero, once you factored in her credit-card debt.

With a sigh Charlotte went back to drinking the last of the coffee, her heart sinking lower than it ever had before.

'Would you like to go out to dinner with me to-night?'

Charlotte's head shot up, blue eyes widening. 'Are you serious?' she said disbelievingly. 'Haven't you been listening? I've just been jilted. My heart's been broken. The last thing I want to do is go out with another good-looking, smooth-talking American who's out here on holiday and who'll say and do anything to get a girl into bed!'

'I'm not American, actually,' he informed her coolly. 'I'm Australian.'

'Huh?'

'I know I sound American,' he elaborated. 'That's because I've been living and working in LA for some years. But I was born in Sydney. My mother married an American, you see, and took us there when I was just a baby. My sister, Beth, was born in the States, but we both went to school here in Australia. Beth stayed on afterwards and is now happily married to a Sydney doctor. Speak of the devil, here she is.'

Charlotte glanced up to see a very pregnant lady waddling towards them. She was not unlike her brother in looks, being tall and striking-looking, with dark hair and eyes. At a guess, Charlotte would have put her age at around thirty, with her brother a few years older.

'I see you haven't changed, brother dear,' she said in a decidedly Australian voice before her laughing eyes went to Charlotte. 'Leave him alone for more than a minute and invariably he'll zero in on the best looking girl for miles. But be warned, darling. He's the love 'em and leave 'em type.'

'Thank you for the recommendation, sister dear,' her brother said drily as he rose to kiss his sister on the cheek. 'I'd introduce you if I knew the lady's name, but she forgot to mention it.'

Charlotte decided this was her cue to escape before she did something stupid, like tell him her name and agree to go to dinner with him tonight. She'd had enough of the love 'em and leave 'em types to last her a lifetime.

Rising to her feet, she hooked her bag over her shoulder and flashed a somewhat brittle smile at him. 'Thanks for the coffee, but I should be going.' And she was off in the direction of the exit, striding out as quickly as she could in her high-heeled, backless sandals.

She should have known he would not let her get away that easily.

'Wait!' he called out, and raced after her. 'Don't take any notice of my sister. She was only joking.'

She stopped and threw him a cynical glance. 'Are you saying you're not of the love 'em and leave 'em variety?'

Charlotte glimpsed the flash of guilt in his eyes before he could hide it.

'Right,' she said, and went to move on again.

'At least tell me your name.'

She stopped again to stare up into his handsome face.

Bad mistake.

His eyes had gone back to hot and hungry. Suddenly, she wanted to tell him her name *and* her phone number; wanted to say yes, I'll go out to dinner with you. But to do so would be the ultimate of foolishnesses. At thirty-three, it was time she stopped being a fool where men were concerned.

'I...I don't think so,' she said, but unconvincingly.

Before she could say boo, he'd whipped out a business card and Biro.

'The numbers on this are irrelevant whilst I'm here,' he said as he balanced the card in his left palm and wrote something on it. 'But I'll put my new mobile number on the back. Or you can call me at my sister's place. Her name's Beth Harvey. She's married to Dr Vincent Harvey. He's an orthopoedic surgeon. They live in Rose Bay and I'll be staying with them for the next fortnight. They're in the phone book. Call me if you change your mind,' he said, and pressed the card into her hand. 'You're upset at the moment, but you know and I know that you didn't really love that Gary guy.'

Their eyes clashed again. Her feminine antennae didn't just twitch this time. They twanged.

'What do you mean?' she asked breathlessly.

'You know what I mean, beautiful,' he returned.

Charlotte opened her mouth to deny any such knowledge. But she couldn't. Because she knew exactly what he meant. How could she have been in love with Gary when *this* man could make her more aware of being a woman than any man ever had? Her heart was racing and the entire surface of her skin felt as if it was on fire.

She glanced down at the card he'd given her, partly out of curiosity, but mostly to escape those unnervingly magnetic and seductive eyes.

His name was Daniel Bannister. And he was a lawyer, with offices in LA.

Charlotte laughed. She couldn't help it. Oh, the irony of it all!

'What's so funny?' he asked.

She looked up, her expression quite cynical. 'Gary

was from LA as well. I think I've had enough of LA lawyers, don't you?'

And, shoving the card back into his hand, she whirled on her high heels and fled.

CHAPTER FOUR

'Look, I'm truly sorry, OK?' Beth apologised. 'I didn't mean any harm. I didn't lie, either. You *are* the love 'em and leave 'em type. Or so you keep telling me.'

Her brother had hardly spoken to her during the drive back from the airport. Or in the two hours since. As soon as they arrived at the house, he'd taken himself off to the guest suite, where he'd showered and changed, after which he'd settled himself on the back terrace and read the morning paper from beginning to end in frosty silence.

Vince had already left for the surgery by their return, and wouldn't be home till at least seven tonight, so Beth had the unpleasant prospect of entertaining Mr Grumpy all day by herself. She was almost grateful that she had an appointment with her obstetrician later on.

Meanwhile, she refused to put up with her brother's sulking any longer.

'For pity's sake, Daniel, what did you expect, anyway?' she went on when he didn't respond to her apology. 'That the girl would fall from her fiancé's arms into yours in a few minutes flat? You're not that irresistible.'

But as Beth lowered herself gingerly into one of the deck chairs she recalled that even when Daniel had been at school, the opposite sex had found him decidedly irresistible.

Yet he was a much more impressive individual now. His shoulders had filled out and his chest had broadened. His hair, still thick and lustrous, was better groomed these days. His features had sharpened and strengthened. There were a few lines at the corners of his eyes, but they didn't detract from his looks. His face now had a stronger, more lived-in look, and his dark, deeply set eyes carried a wealth of intelligence and worldliness in their depths which women would find mysterious and sexy.

'The trouble with you, Daniel Bannister,' she pronounced irritably, 'is you're too used to getting your own way with the women that take your eye.'

Daniel knew Beth was right. But it didn't make this morning's fiasco any easier to bear. And it didn't really explain why he was so upset.

'I just can't get her out of my mind,' he said, surprising himself when he realised he'd made this admission out loud.

Beth looked startled, too. 'But you only spoke to her for a few minutes.'

'I know.'

'On top of that, she was a blonde.'

Daniel smiled a wry smile. 'Yes, I know. But I really liked this one. She was sweet.'

Beth laughed. 'She was sexy.'

'Not in an obvious way.'

'Oh, come on. With *that* figure?'

Daniel frowned. Yes, he supposed she *was* sexy, and yes, he'd like nothing better than to have the chance to make love to her. But in the time since she'd walked out of his life this morning, it wasn't sex that was on his mind so much as just wanting to be with her again.

'I have to find her,' he pronounced.

'How? You don't even know her name.'

'I know she booked a wedding reception at the Regency Royale hotel tomorrow. I could get her name and number from them.'

'They won't give it to you.'

Daniel nodded determinedly. 'Oh, yes, they will.'

Beth sighed. He was right. They probably would. Daniel had the gift of the gab. He could talk anybody into anything.

'You said you had to go into the city to see your doctor at twelve, didn't you?' he asked.

'Yes.'

'Anywhere near the Regency Royale?'

'A good ten to fifteen minute walk.' Her doctor's rooms were up in Macquarie Street. The Regency was down near the Rocks.

'I'll pop down there whilst you're in the surgery. How long do you think you'll take?'

'Could be anything up to an hour or two if the doctor's called away to deliver a baby. That seems to happen quite a bit.'

'We can keep in touch by phone.'

'Are you sure this is such a good idea, Daniel? I mean, that poor girl would have to be extra-vulnerable right now.'

'I have no intention of hurting her, sis. I just want

to take her out to dinner. Get to know her a bit better.'

Beth rolled her eyes. There was no point in arguing with Daniel. There never was. Once he decided he wanted something, nothing stood in his way.

'I'll book a taxi for eleven-thirty, then. No point in driving into town. Parking is a pain.'

Charlotte pulled up at the entrance to the Regency Royale just after noon. Although twelve-thirty was the time she'd arranged to meet her mum and dad for lunch, she knew that her ultra-punctual, always-leave-plenty-of-time-to-spare parents were sure to have arrived in Sydney early, and would already be sitting there in the lobby, waiting for her. She had contemplated being late but then decided it was far better to get her bad news over and done with as soon as possible.

The hours since returning home from the airport had been difficult, with recriminations and regrets. But mostly filled with tears.

Maybe if Louise had been there, she'd have been able to maintain her equilibrium by having a bitching session about Gary's betrayal. But Louise had had to go to work. Whereas *she* was on a week's holiday from today, courtesy of her supposed wedding tomorrow. They virtually passed each other in the foyer of their old apartment building, with Louise giving her a quick hug before making Charlotte promise not to ring that bastard, Gary. An easy promise to give, and to keep. She couldn't have borne to even talk to him, let alone listen to his pathetic excuses and apologies.

The effect of their empty flat was undermining in the extreme, a huge wave of depression descending within seconds of Charlotte letting herself in through the front door. The silence was awful—plus the sight of the snaps of herself and Gary taken at the airport which she kept on the bookcase in the hallway. She threw them all in the bin, then threw herself on her bed and wept in a wild mixture of bitterness, anger and despair.

After an hour or so, she pulled herself together to have some breakfast and to send an email back to Gary telling him what she thought of him and that he was to never, ever contact her again!

The moment she sent it, however, she burst into tears again.

This time, she pulled herself together reasonably quickly and made a few necessary cancellation calls. The formal-clothes hire place. The celebrant. The florist. And finally, the suite she'd booked for their wedding night.

By this point, she was too upset to cancel the whole reception as well. She decided to do that later in the day, in person, after she'd talked to her parents. Maybe she could talk the hotel into giving her father some kind of refund.

The physical damage of her three crying jags had not been easy to repair. An ice pack had helped, plus some carefully applied make-up. She'd changed her clothes as well, her outfit this morning having been chosen with Gary in mind. Now she was wearing tailored cream trousers and a red shirt with three-quarter-length sleeves. Fawn pumps. Straw bag. Red lipstick.

'Will you be booking into the hotel, ma'am?' the parking valet asked when she climbed out of her car.

Charlotte suppressed a groan over the 'ma'am'. Since when had she become a ma'am and not a miss? Still, the valet attendant looked all of nineteen, if that, so she supposed, at thirty-three, she was a ma'am to him.

Depressing, though, and not what she needed today.

'No,' she said, forcing a smile as she handed the fellow the keys to her silver Kia Rio. 'Just meeting someone here for lunch,' she added.

'You'll need a parking ticket, then, ma'am.'

Taking the ticket from him, she whirled and pushed through the revolving glass doors into the huge, airy arcade which led to the hotel proper.

A right trap for tourists and guests, this arcade, Charlotte thought as she strode past the exclusive boutiques which sold designer clothes, fabulous jewellery and the sexiest of lingerie. A trap for brides-to-be as well, she recalled with a sigh, thinking of the money she'd spent in the lingerie shop the last time she'd been in here.

Charlotte promptly veered to the other side of the arcade, where there was nothing to provoke depressing memories, just a couple of doorways. The first led into the Rendezvous bar, a trendy bar she'd visited once or twice with Louise. The second led into the bistro-style bar and grill called the Tavern, which she'd checked out the last time she'd been here and where she intended taking her parents for lunch. They served good old-fashioned pub and club meals, just the thing for a country couple who weren't partial to à la carte cuisine.

'Can't stand fancy food,' her father always said.

Charlotte's stomach churned as she thought of her father. More so when she reached the end of the arcade and stepped from the marble floor onto the plush carpet of the hotel lobby. Just the sight of the decor in there reminded her how expensive a wedding reception here was, even one which was only having fifty guests. The cake alone had cost a bomb!

Charlotte's only comfort was that she'd decided on only the one bridesmaid. If one of her sisters hadn't been pregnant there would have been two more!

But oh…how she wished she'd taken notice of Gary when he'd requested a really small wedding. That would have made what she was about to do a little easier. Bad enough that she had to tell her parents she wasn't getting married. Worse that her dad had wasted all that money which he could have put to far better use.

The ongoing drought over the last decade had not hit the family as hard as some, but things were still tough. The money her wedding had cost would have replaced the breeding stock her dad had been forced to sell this past year. Or put in an extra dam. Or taken her parents on that cruise they were always talking about going on but which they never got round to having.

She'd thought how tired and old they were looking at Christmas.

Charlotte glanced around the lobby with an ever-tightening stomach. But her parents weren't there. She turned full circle, her gaze checking every corner of the reception area. The place wasn't remotely crowded at this time of day. Too late to be booking out. Too early to be booking in.

No. They definitely weren't there.

She might have rung them if they'd had a mobile phone, check if they'd become lost once they hit the city. But of course her parents hadn't come into the twenty-first century yet. Probably never would.

Charlotte settled herself down on one of the deep, velvet-covered armchairs to wait, her body facing the entrance from the arcade. That was the way her folks would come.

She almost didn't recognise him at first. He wasn't wearing the same clothes he'd been wearing this morning. His expensive grey suit had been replaced by dark blue jeans and a navy polo shirt trimmed with white. A pair of sunglasses was perched on top of his head. Navy and white trainers covered his feet.

It had taken an effort of will for Charlotte to put Mr Daniel Bannister out of her mind after she'd left the airport this morning, though once she arrived home more immediate and pressing events had over-taken her. Now, suddenly, there he was again, as disturbingly sexy as ever.

Charlotte's jolt of shock had her sucking in air, and immediately his head turned in her direction. He seemed just as startled to see *her*. But pleased.

Oh, yes, definitely pleased.

Charlotte's back stiffened against the armchair as he started walking towards her. At the last moment, she rose to her feet, rather than stay seated. Too awkward having to look up so far into those incredible eyes.

He whipped the sunglasses off his head during his approach, folding and popping them into his chest pocket, his mouth broadening into a dazzling smile at the same time, showing perfectly straight white teeth and a dimple in one cheek.

As if he wasn't attractive enough already.

'I don't believe it!' he exclaimed. 'I came here hoping to pry your name and number out of the hotel staff, and here you are in the flesh.'

All the breath rushed out of Charlotte's lungs at his admission. This wasn't an amazing coincidence. He was actively pursuing her.

Fury warred with flattery till she was simply flustered.

'I told you I was meeting my parents here for lunch,' she said, her face going hot once more. What was it about this man that made her act and feel like some silly teenager in front of her favourite pop star?

'Really? Can't say I recall you mentioning it. If you had, I would have remembered. But no matter. You're here. Now I have the opportunity to redress the bad impression my sister must have given you of me this morning.'

'You just don't know how to take no for an answer, do you?' she threw at him.

He grinned. 'Beth said as much when I told her I

had to find you. She's here in town, seeing her doctor, so I set out on my mission to uncover the identity of the lovely lady I met this morning, and whom I haven't stopped thinking about since.'

'You are the most annoying man,' Charlotte declared, even as she coloured some more. Couldn't he understand that the last thing she wanted and needed today was more evidence of how stupid she'd been, thinking she was in love with Gary?

It was mortifying, the way her eyes kept gobbling him up. Dear heaven, but he *was* gorgeous.

She couldn't help wishing that it had been *this* LA lawyer she'd run into on the Gold Coast last year. Because he wouldn't have taken any notice of her romantically. He'd have seduced her on the spot, then happily dumped her the next day. He wouldn't have lied to her and betrayed her and jilted her.

Men like Daniel didn't have to con women to get them into bed. The silly fools would be only too ready to do whatever he wanted without a single promise, herself included.

This was the most flustering part of her feelings right now. That she, Charlotte Gale, a just-jilted woman, could be wanting any man the way she was suddenly wanting the man standing right in front of her.

'I'm still not going out to dinner with you tonight,' she pronounced tartly.

'That's OK,' he replied without missing a beat. 'Tomorrow night will do just as well. Or the next night. I'm here in Sydney for a fortnight.'

'You're not listening again. I said no. Now I'm

saying it again. I don't want to go out to dinner with you. Ever.'

'You don't mean that.'

She did. But he wasn't getting the message.

'Some things are meant to be, beautiful. Otherwise why would fate have put you here, just waiting for me?'

Charlotte groaned. 'I wasn't waiting for *you*. I was waiting for my parents. I told you. They... Oh—' She broke off, her head still spinning with the effort of trying to gain some control over herself and the situation. 'They're here.'

CHAPTER FIVE

DANIEL turned to see a couple who had country written all over them coming across the lobby in their direction. Both looked in their mid to late sixties, the woman plump with short grey hair, the man also grey-haired, but rake-thin with a weather-beaten face and kind blue eyes. Both had probably once been quite handsome. They had good features. Both were wearing suits and looked uncomfortable in them.

'Charlotte!' the woman exclaimed as she hurried forward to give her daughter a peck on the cheek.

Daniel smiled. At least now he knew her name. Charlotte. Great name for a great girl. She was going to take some talking around, he could see. But he was *not* going to take no for an answer.

Daniel was well versed in body language. And in the contrariness of women. Charlotte was as attracted to him as he was to her. Her relationship with that pathetic Gary guy had been one big romantic illusion. And she knew it. He'd seen the realisation in her eyes this morning.

Of course, he understood she was still upset. No woman liked to be dumped, especially the day before her wedding. She also clearly loved her parents and didn't want to disappoint them. Or tell them that they'd wasted a whole heap of cash on a wedding which wasn't going to take place. Once she broke the bad news to them, she was going to need some comforting.

'And dear Gary!' Charlotte's mother suddenly whirled to give him a big bear hug before putting him from her at arm's length and looking him over from top to toe. 'My, but you're even better looking than in your photos. Of course, you had sunglasses on in those so I couldn't see your eyes. You didn't tell me Gary had such beautiful eyes, Charlotte.'

Charlotte, Daniel could see, was dumbstruck. He was pretty flabbergasted himself.

But of course, it was a logical mistake for her mother to make. Charlotte had made it herself this morning. Which was another reason he knew Charlotte was attracted to him. She must have a certain physical type she liked.

'The thing is, Mum,' Charlotte finally blurted out, 'he's n—'

'He's a damn fine-looking man all round,' her father broke in, taking Daniel's hand and pumping it enthusiastically in both of his. 'Tomorrow is going to be the happiest day of my life, seeing my baby girl finally married to a man worthy of her. I have to tell you, Gary, that her last boyfriend was a right drongo. But she's finally come up trumps!'

'Dad, for pity's sake!' Charlotte wailed.

'You told me there were no secrets between you and Gary here. You said you'd told him all about Dwayne. Do you know he even wore an earring?' he directed at Daniel with a truly pained expression. 'Real men don't wear earrings!'

'I certainly don't.' Daniel had tried one once but he thought he looked a right prat.

'I noticed that. You're my kind of man, Gary. Welcome to the family.' And he pumped his hand some more.

Daniel wished at that moment that he *were* Gary. He hated having to disappoint them almost as much as Charlotte did.

When a wild but brilliant idea popped into his mind, Daniel embraced it immediately. It would kill two birds with one stone.

'It's a pleasure to meet you at last, sir,' he said. 'And you too, Mrs—er...' Damn it all, he didn't know their surname. 'Would you mind if I called you Mum and Dad?' he improvised.

'Not at all, my boy!' Charlotte's father beamed. So did her mother.

Charlotte just stared at him, her mouth still dangling open a little. But she didn't make a move to tell them the truth, he noticed.

'Always wanted a son-in-law to call me Dad,' her father raved on, having at last returned Daniel's hand. 'John—that's Lizzie's husband—he at least calls us Peter and Betty. But Keith—that's Alice's husband—he still calls us Mr and Mrs Gale.'

Daniel absorbed all this information for future reference.

'Ga-ry.'

Daniel was startled when Charlotte spoke up, the sweet smile on her face belying the dark irony in her eyes, and in her voice. 'Could I have a moment?

Mum. Dad. There's something I need to discuss privately with Gary. Would you mind?'

'That's all right, love,' her father said. 'We'll be back shortly. Give you two lovebirds time enough to sort out whatever it is you have to sort out.'

'What in hell do you think you're doing?' Charlotte hissed under her breath as soon as her parents were far enough away.

'I guess I'm going to marry you tomorrow,' Daniel returned evenly, unable to stop a smile from pulling at his mouth.

'Don't be ridiculous!'

'Look, it won't be legal,' he reassured her calmly. 'But it'll stop your parents from having a really rotten day today. And tomorrow. You might feel a whole lot better, too. You look seriously stressed out, Charlotte.'

She was shaking her head in continued disbelief.

'You're insane!'

'Absolutely not. I'm a lot of things but insane is not one of them.'

'But we can't possibly get away with it!'

'Yes, we can. Your parents already believe I'm Gary. Everyone else will, too.'

'Louise won't. She knows Gary didn't show up.'

Louise. Daniel searched his excellent memory bank and retrieved Louise from their conversation this morning. 'Isn't she supposed to be your best friend?'

'Yes.'

'Then tell her the truth and ask her to go along with it.'

'But…but I've already cancelled things!' she protested.

'What things?'

'The celebrant for starters, and the flowers, and the tux rental, and…and…'

'Nothing that can't be sorted out.' Though the celebrant could stay cancelled, Daniel decided. He'd find someone else to act as a celebrant. As a lawyer, he couldn't risk being guilty of any kind of fraud.

Vince would probably do it. For a doctor, he was somewhat of a thrill-seeker. Went skydiving for fun.

'You haven't cancelled the reception yet, have you?' he rapped out.

'No.'

'Where's the ceremony itself taking place? Not a church obviously, if you were having a celebrant.'

'Here, in the hotel.'

'No problems there, then.'

'You *are* crazy,' she muttered under her breath.

'Crazy about you, beautiful.'

She stared up at him, stunned by the speed with which he'd arranged things, and taken advantage of his similarity to Gary.

Not that he was really like Gary.

'I've never met a man like you,' she said dazedly. 'I'll bet you wouldn't romance a girl over the internet, ask her to marry you and then not show up.'

'No, Charlotte, I definitely wouldn't. Aside from being allergic to real marriages as opposed to pretend ones, I can't stand the internet. Waste of time except for business reasons, and *very* bad for the eyes.'

She laughed. She couldn't help it. This whole situation was bizarre. And it was whilst she was laughing that he pulled her into his arms and kissed her, right there, in the hotel lobby. In front of everyone.

At thirty-three, Charlotte had been kissed many times before. But this man kissed the same way he'd looked at her at the airport this morning. With a passion and intensity that was mind-blowing. His arms were wrapped tightly around her, his mouth white-hot on hers. She could feel herself dissolving under the sizzling brand of his lips. Not just her body, but also her mind. When his tongue joined in, every ounce of will-power she owned melted right away, replaced by the desire to surrender herself totally to what he wanted.

He wanted to pretend to marry her tomorrow? Fine.

He wanted her to go to dinner with him tonight? OK.

He wanted to take her to bed afterwards? Yes, please.

Her father noisily clearing his throat had Charlotte finally surfacing from her liquid state to the real world. Once she stepped back out of Daniel's arms, some semblance of common sense returned. But the smouldering inner heat he'd generated remained, teasing her with the thought that maybe this man could do for her what no man ever had before…

Charlotte tried not to blush at this thought, whilst Daniel looked highly satisfied with the situation. His mission had been accomplished.

Charlotte knew he wasn't doing this for her parents' happiness. Or for hers. He was doing it to put her in his debt, and in his bed.

Not that he had to go to such amazing lengths. She would have gone to bed with him, anyway.

Twenty-four hours ago, Charlotte would have scorned anyone who said she would ever be a pushover. The fact she was prepared to say yes to Daniel Bannister within hours of meeting him was as shocking to her as it was intriguing.

Why him?

Was it his movie-star looks? His charm? His intelligence? Or was it the power of *his* desire that was seducing and compelling her? Men had desired her before but never quite like this. This was something else.

Her cheeks continued to burn as her eyes met his, her heart-rate having not yet calmed. If she felt like this after a kiss, then how would she feel once she was in bed with him, their bodies totally naked, his flesh inside hers?

A quiver rippled down her spine at the thought, her heart flipping right over when he slid an intimate arm around her waist and pulled her back against him.

Daniel resumed the conversation. 'Charlotte was confessing to me that you'd all organised a bigger wedding for us than we'd originally planned.'

'Yes, well, I couldn't give my youngest daughter a lesser wedding than my other daughters, could I?' her father pronounced proudly, reminding Charlotte why she'd been sick with worry over disappointing her darling dad. She would be forever grateful to

Daniel that she didn't have to now, regardless of his ulterior motives.

Of course, it was still going to be awkward at a later date, explaining why her loving husband had to go back to the States, then extremely disappointing for her to confess that their marriage hadn't worked out.

But she would cross that bridge when she came to it.

For now, her mum and dad were smiling. That was all that mattered.

'Do you think we might get along to the restaurant, daughter?' her dad said. 'Haven't had a bite since breakfast.'

'I'm hungry too,' Daniel said with a wicked glance at Charlotte.

The man was a devil, no doubt about it. But it was impossible not to like him, as well as want him. He must have cut a right swathe through the ladies in LA these past few years, Charlotte reckoned. That combination of magnetism, machismo and manners was lethally attractive.

'I hope we're not going to one of those places where they take hours to serve you,' her father said with a frown.

'Amen to that,' Daniel agreed. 'When I'm hungry, I have to be fed quickly.'

Charlotte cocked an eyebrow, just to show him she was well aware what he was up to with his *double entendres*. Then she shot him a sickeningly sarcastic smile. 'I had a feeling you'd say that. Don't worry, Dad, the bistro is just a short walk away. You boys could have a beer while we're waiting for our meal. And, Mum, you could have a sherry. Or some white wine, if you'd prefer.'

'A sherry would be lovely,' her mother said, the warm approval on her face giving Charlotte a real buzz.

Charlotte rarely received her mother's approval, unlike her two older sisters, who hadn't put a foot wrong in their lives. They'd both done well at school. Both had married their childhood sweethearts, sons of local farmers. Both had produced children.

Charlotte, by contrast, hadn't finished school, had never learned to cook, couldn't take up a hem, regularly forgot important dates and, till recently, was yet to find a husband.

As a child, she'd often been described as difficult. And a dreamer.

'Her head is always in the clouds,' she had heard her mother say to Aunt Gladys one day when she was about thirteen. 'I don't know what's going to become of her.'

What became of her was she bolted for the city when she was a couple of months shy of her sixteenth birthday, having secretly applied for and secured a hairdressing apprenticeship advertised in the *Sydney Morning Herald*. Her distraught parents weren't able to force her to return home, or to finish her school certificate, because she was able to support herself. In the end, they stopped trying to convince Charlotte she was too young to live away from home in the big city.

Actually, hairdressing was just a means to an end.

Her heart's desire was to see what the world had to offer outside of farm life and country boys. Sydney was an eye-opener but soon it too was limiting. So when Charlotte finished her apprenticeship, she began a series of jobs on ships that cruised all over the world.

By the time she was twenty-five, she'd been everywhere an ocean liner could take her. By then, she'd grown a bit bored with ship life and decided to try working in some of the world's luxury resorts.

Over the next few years, Charlotte worked mostly in Asia, but also in the South Pacific, on various tropical islands. She then did a brief stint in a top hotel in London, but had found the climate not to her liking. She also found herself suffering, surprisingly, from homesickness, something which astounded her.

So, shortly before her thirtieth birthday, Charlotte returned to Australia, where she spent a few wonderfully restful weeks with her folks on the farm before realising, rather reluctantly this time, that country life was still not for her. What she *was* craving, she discovered, was a more settled existence. She wanted to put down roots. Wanted a boyfriend who lasted longer than a few months. She wanted marriage, and children. Possibly even a house with a garden.

Charlotte was blown away by this last bit. Miss Wanderlust herself wanting what most Australian girls wanted. Amazing!

Not one to ever shirk from a goal, Charlotte set about achieving what she wanted with a passion. She returned to Sydney, got herself a job and a flat, then set about doing what girls of her age did when they were on the lookout for Mr Right. She made friends with all the single girls she worked with—networking was crucial. She went to all the right bars with them on a Friday night. She smiled at every available-looking guy. And—most important of all—she joined a gym.

Which was where she met Dwayne, one of their personal trainers. Dwayne made it obvious right from the start that he fancied her. Within two weeks they were dating. Within four he coerced her into bed with words of undying love. Within six they were living together.

But that was where their relationship stagnated for the next two years. Dwayne was not ready, he said, for marriage and kiddies just yet. He was only twenty-eight. But he hinted a proposal was definitely on the cards once he reached thirty. So Charlotte clung on, despite becoming aware that they rarely talked any more, their sex life had dwindled to once a week, and Dwayne was working late more nights than ever.

She should not have been shocked by his dumping her for another girl. What shocked her was the speed with which he married his new, already pregnant girlfriend.

Charlotte was left to wonder what the gym bunny had that she didn't have. She couldn't help thinking that the answer wasn't the other girl's blonde hair, but her sexual know-how.

'Charlotte. Is this the place you were talking about?'

Her mother's voice cut through Charlotte's reverie, shocking her back to the present. Blinking a bit blankly for a second or two, she discovered they were standing outside the entrance to the bistro. She must have walked there on automatic pilot whilst she daydreamed.

'Yes, yes, it is. Sorry. Just wool-gathering as usual.'

Her mother smiled indulgently. 'That's all right. A girl's allowed some wool-gathering the day before her wedding. Most brides are a bit nervous.'

Her father laughed. 'Nervous? Our Charlie? That'll be the day. She's just excited.'

Excited…

Charlotte glanced up into Daniel's dark eyes, which glittered back down at her.

'Just a tad,' she confessed with considerable understatement. 'Come on, let's get you in here to eat.'

Taking her mother's elbow, she ushered her into the bistro. Daniel and her dad trailed after them, chatting away as if they'd been best mates for years.

'Have you decided what you might like to eat yet?' she asked her mother after the woman had spent several minutes perusing all the options. Daniel and her dad had already ordered steaks, medium rare. Men, Charlotte had always found, were more decisive with food than women. She herself didn't feel like eating at all. Stress always doused her appetite. Excitement, too.

She'd had more than enough of both for one day.

Her mother continued to dither whilst Daniel proceeded to the bar to order the drinks. Beer for the men. Cream sherry for her mother and a dry white wine for herself.

Meanwhile, her dad claimed a booth-style table for them next to one of the wide windows that overlooked the city street outside.

In the end, both her mother and Charlotte ordered the same as the men, though they chose smaller steaks and ordered them well done. Their drinks had arrived by the time they sat down. Charlotte immediately swooped up her glass and was having some soothing sips of the crisply chilled wine when a mobile phone started ringing.

Charlotte knew it wasn't hers. Wrong tune.

It was Daniel's.

CHAPTER SIX

'EXCUSE me, everyone,' Daniel said as he fished his slimline cellphone out of his back pocket, flipped it open and put it to his ear.

Charlotte gave him a slight dig in the ribs, reminding him he'd have to be careful what he said.

'Hi there,' seemed safe enough.

'Beth here. I'm finally finished with the doc. Everything's fine, though I've put on another damned kilo. So where are you and how did things go? Did you find out her name?'

'I'm having lunch with Charlotte and her folks right now,' he replied, hoping that would floor his sister into silence.

He was right. It did.

'Don't worry about me,' he went on hurriedly. 'I'll take a taxi back to your place after we're finished, though that might not be for a while. Arrangements to make, et cetera. Thanks for calling. See you later. Ciao.'

Turning his mobile right off to stop any further awkward calls from Beth, he slipped it in his pocket, vowing to give her a call back as soon as he had the chance.

'Sorry about that,' he said brightly. 'It was the lady whose place I'm staying at tonight. She and her husband are friends of friends of mine. I didn't think it would be right to stay at Charlotte's place. Not the night before the wedding, anyway.'

'Are these people coming to the wedding tomorrow, Charlotte?' Betty Gale asked her daughter.

'Er—'

'No, they're not,' Daniel jumped in. 'I didn't ask them. I didn't realise it was going to be such a big wedding, remember?'

'But that's not right,' Mr Gale said. 'They should come. Charlotte, surely something could be arranged.'

Charlotte groaned inside. 'I don't think so, Dad. The numbers for the reception were finalised a couple of days ago.' The last thing she wanted was to cost her dad *more* money.

'Please don't concern yourselves,' Daniel said swiftly. 'They really wouldn't expect to come.'

'If you say so, Gary.'

Charlotte winced. How she hated hearing them call him Gary! Daniel was a much nicer name.

Their meals arrived. Charlotte only picked at hers, her mind drifting back to names.

Daniel. Daniel Bannister. *Mrs* Daniel Bannister.

'You're not dieting, are you, darling?' Daniel suddenly asked her.

Her sharp intake of breath reflected the shock produced by her own foolish thoughts, *not* by his calling her darling. She knew he was only acting. No way was she really his darling, or anything close. Yet there *she* was, fantasising about being married to him.

God, she was hopeless. Hadn't this fiasco with

Gary taught her anything? Talk about jumping from the frying pan into the fire. If she started imagining she was falling for Daniel, she needed her head read. OK, so he was utterly gorgeous-looking and incredibly sexy, with the kind of powerful and dynamic personality you usually only read about.

Charlotte had no doubt he would be very good in bed.

But he wasn't good at love. Or commitment. He couldn't have made his intentions clearer. He said he was allergic to marriage, and his own sister had called him the love 'em and leave 'em type.

Common sense demanded she not weave any romantic fantasies around him. He was not some knight in shining armour. His aim hadn't been rescuing her damsel in distress, but seducing her.

She had to keep that fact in the forefront of her mind during the next couple of days or she'd end up crying a whole lot more than she had about Gary.

'Charlotte never eats much when she's nervous,' her mother answered for her, which brought a grateful smile from Charlotte. She put down her knife and fork, picked up a chip with her fingers and nibbled on it.

'I'm just the opposite,' Daniel said. 'I eat like a horse when I'm nervous.' And he forked a large piece of steak into his mouth.

'I can't imagine you ever being nervous,' Charlotte said with a dry laugh.

'You'd be surprised,' he returned.

Charlotte wouldn't mind betting he'd never suffered a crisis of confidence in his entire life, whereas she'd spent most of hers not even knowing what she wanted out of life. Even when she thought she did, her life had still lurched from one disaster to the next.

'Everyone gets nervous occasionally,' her father joined in. 'Caring makes any man nervous. I was nervous when I married your mother. And each time she was expecting. I dare say I'll be nervous again when you and Gary have a little one.'

The threat of tears came out of nowhere. Charlotte knew she would not be able to explain them, so she had to get out of there. At least for a minute or two.

She dropped the rest of the chip and stood up abruptly. 'Sorry. Have to go the ladies'. The wine.'

Bolting for the powder room did the trick. Not only did it stop the tears, but it also gave her the opportunity to call Louise.

'Goodness knows what she's going to say,' Charlotte muttered as she raced into a cubicle and punched in Louise's work number.

The owner of the hairdressing place Louise worked at didn't like her taking personal calls, especially on a Friday, but this was an emergency. It took a while before she came on the line, during which Charlotte's already over-active stomach did the tango.

'Yes?' Louise asked agitatedly.

'Louise, it's Charlotte. You haven't told anyone about what happened with Gary this morning, have you?'

'No. Why?'

'Not even Brad?' Brad was Louise's boyfriend and the best man.

'Haven't had the opportunity. I was going to tell him tonight. We're meeting for drinks after work.'

'Thank heaven, because the wedding's back on.'

'What? *How?* Did Gary ditch the PA and take a later plane or something?'

Charlotte told her what had transpired in broad strokes.

'Now, don't say a single word,' Charlotte warned before her friend could launch into a torrent of protest. 'This is a done deed and nothing you say will stop me, so don't waste your breath.'

'Fine by me. It's your life. Besides, this Daniel sounds a darn sight more interesting than Gary. He really came gunning for you, huh? Must be seriously smitten. I suppose he has to be reasonably good-looking, if he looks like Gary. Not that I thought Gary was all that hot in his photos.'

'Makes Gary look lukewarm.'

'Oho, he's not the only one who's smitten. I always said you didn't love Gary. And vice versa.'

'Yes, I know. But this isn't love, Louise.'

'Don't tell you've finally fallen in *lust* with a man?'

Louise had a way of cutting to the chase about things, especially on the subject of sex. Lust was not a word Charlotte liked but *lustful* certainly described most of the thoughts Daniel engendered in her.

'Possibly.'

'About time too. Look, we'll talk more tonight. Alvira is looking daggers at me, so I'd better go. You will be coming home some time tonight, won't you?'

'Yes, of course,' Charlotte said, and meant it.

Daniel was going to have to wait till tomorrow night to have his wicked way with her. No way was she going to jump into bed with him tonight, no matter how much she might want to. A girl had to have some pride!

Her return to the table was greeted by a questioning glance from Daniel. But she could hardly tell him anything till the lunch was over and her parents had checked into their room in the hotel.

Fortunately, after lunch her mum and dad were happy enough to look after themselves for the rest of the day.

Charlotte sighed a rather weary sigh as soon as the lift doors shut on her parents.

'You sound tired,' Daniel said.

'I *am* tired.'

'In that case I'll let you off dinner tonight. Far better you go home and have a good night's rest.'

'I never said I'd *have* dinner with you tonight,' she reminded him tartly.

'The girl who kissed me in the lobby would have come to dinner with me if I'd asked again.'

'*You* kissed *me*!'

'Don't be pedantic. You liked me kissing you. A lot.'

'Good grief, you're impossible!'

'And you're irresistible.'

She laughed. 'Not according to my last two boyfriends.'

'They were fools. I'm not.'

'I only have your word for that. So why *are* you doing this for me tomorrow, Daniel?' she asked him, determined to have him put his cards on the table. 'Or perhaps more to the point, why did you chase after me the way you did? The truth, please. I've had enough of men telling me lies.'

He shrugged. 'Impossible to analyse some things. When I first saw you this morning, it was like being struck by a bolt of lightning. I've never felt that way about a woman before, especially a blonde.'

Charlotte was both flattered and taken aback. 'You don't like blondes?'

'Let's just say they usually set off bad memories for me. After my father left my mother, his subsequent wives have all been blondes.'

'His *wives*! How many has he had?'

'Five, including my mother, at last count. But what the heck? He's only sixty-five. Plenty of time yet for a few more.'

The bitterness in Daniel's voice brought some understanding as to why he might be allergic to marriage, whereas Charlotte had had nothing but good examples of people being married. Her parents. Her aunts and uncles. Her sisters. All happy with their partners. Divorce was unheard-of in her family.

Suddenly she wanted to know more about the man who was going to pretend to marry her tomorrow. A whole lot more.

'How about we go for a cup of coffee somewhere?' she suggested. 'We really need to talk.'

He smiled that sexy smile of his. 'We really need to do a whole lot of things. But you're right. Talking would be a good idea for now. But somewhere very public, please. So that I can keep my hands off you.

Kissing you before did dreadful things to me. If I hadn't been able to distract myself with food I don't know what I would have done.'

Charlotte found herself laughing again. 'You're a wicked man, do you know that?'

Daniel didn't know that. He had his shortcomings but he'd never thought of himself as wicked. Still, her comment made him try to do what he'd just said couldn't be done. Analyse his feelings for Charlotte.

Was it just sexual desire for her which had propelled and compelled his actions today? Was he going through with this pretend wedding, just to get her into bed?

Absolutely not. He could have got her into bed anyway. The way she'd responded to his kiss had told him that. He was doing what he was doing because he genuinely liked her. And genuinely liked her folks. They were the warmest, nicest family he'd ever met and he hated to think of them in distress.

But perhaps it was for the best if he didn't tell her that. Best she think he *was* wicked. The thought seemed to amuse her. And turn her on. Turning her on was good. Having her fall in love with him on the rebound was not.

Daniel didn't want to take up where Gary had left off.

That would be cruel.

Charlotte had to be extra-vulnerable right now. Still, she wasn't some young naive girl. She was a woman, a beautiful sexy woman with needs. It had been eight months since she'd been with a man. Daniel had been without a woman in his bed too.

High time they both had some comfort.

The prospect of spending their 'wedding night' together tomorrow was going to keep him awake tonight, that was for sure. Thinking of their wedding night, however, brought another idea, one which he would attend to before leaving the hotel.

'Where do you want to go for coffee?' he asked.

'We could walk down to one of the cafés on the quay. Then I could take you to the clothes-hire place on the way. It's not far from here. We need to rent a tux for you.'

'No need. I have a tux. Never go anywhere without one.' He'd been caught short once when he'd gone to Boston to visit friends.

Charlotte frowned. 'What kind?'

'Black. Single-breasted. Satin lapels. A white dress shirt and a black bow-tie. Will that do?'

'Perfect,' she said. 'That's one less expense. And one less job to do. Now all I have to do is let the florist know the wedding's back on, plus the celebrant.'

'You can call the florist but forget the celebrant. We can't have a real one, Charlotte. Too risky, legally. I'll get someone to stand in and play the part. My brother-in-law will do it. The bridal suite can be real, though.'

'The bridal suite?' she choked out.

Their eyes locked, hers wide, his narrowed.

Daniel was momentarily thrown by the sudden

panic he glimpsed there. Surely she must have realised that was where tomorrow would end.

'You said you'd cancelled it,' he reminded her.

'I…I didn't actually book one of the bridal suites,'
she said, clearly flustered. 'They have several here in
the hotel, each one decorated with a different theme.
They're all terribly expensive. I couldn't afford any
of them so I booked one of the ordinary suites.'

'I see. Well, you don't have to worry about the
expense any more. My treat. You ring the florist
whilst I go organise one of those suites. Then we'll
have that coffee. I think a walk in the fresh air would
do us both good.'

Ten minutes later they were walking together down
George Street towards the quay. The day had become
a little hotter, but not unpleasantly so. Charlotte had
had no trouble re-booking the florist, with Daniel
looking similarly pleased.

She didn't dare ask him what suite he'd booked.
She didn't want to think about tomorrow night. She
would think about that tomorrow.

'You handled the situation with your parents very
well,' Daniel complimented when they stopped at a
corner for a red light. 'No one would have known
you were upset. Which you must be. I'm not that
insensitive that I don't realise today has been very
difficult for you.'

Difficult in more ways than one. How often did
one man dump you and another bewitch you within
the space of a few hours?

'Training,' she said brusquely, which led to her

telling him about her work history and how she'd learned not to wear her heart on her sleeve.

'Except when I've just been jilted,' she added as the light turned green and they walked on. 'I always lose it on occasions like that. Especially when I find out the man who's supposedly in love with me has made some other girl pregnant. Would you believe this isn't the first time this has happened?'

'That's incredibly bad luck.'

'I agree,' she said drily, and launched into her sad tale about Dwayne.

Daniel nodded sympathetically at all the right moments.

'Men can be right bastards at times,' he pronounced when she finished.

She stared at him, then smiled. 'You'd know, I guess.'

By this time they'd reached the quay area and weren't far from the open-air café Charlotte was taking him to.

'On the plus side,' she said as they strolled along together, 'you are a wonderful listener.'

'Aah, now, that's *my* training. I'm not just any old lawyer, you see. I'm a divorce lawyer. With female-only clients. A good proportion of my job is just listening to women rave on. I have to confess I'm used to hearing the sexual shortcomings of the male sex. Frankly, some of the horror stories I've heard make me ashamed of being a man at times.'

'But why do you have only female clients? Surely men want you to represent them sometimes.'

'Aah, now, that's a long story.'

Charlotte refused to let him fob her off with that old chestnut. 'You must tell me all about it over coffee,' she said firmly.

Daniel had no intention of doing any such thing, but oddly enough, within ten minutes of their sitting down together at one of the very pleasant alfresco tables, he found himself telling her in minute detail all about his father's desertion and subsequent marriages.

'Mom never recovered from his betrayal,' he said as he stirred his coffee. 'And I guess neither did I. Beth was too young to hate him. She never even knew him. But I despise the man for what he did, and what he's done since. When I first started practising law and handling divorces, I did have male clients. But I couldn't put my heart into representing them. It felt like I was representing my father. When I became a partner in the practice a few years back, I decided enough was enough. I've only had women clients from then on.'

'I fully understand,' Charlotte sympathised. 'And your mother? How is she coping these days?'

Daniel's chest tightened. 'Mom passed away last year.'

'Oh, how dreadful for you!' Charlotte exclaimed with genuine sympathy in her gorgeous blue eyes. 'I don't know what I'd do if my mother died. I'd be devastated. And of course so were you. I can see it in your face.'

Daniel blinked his amazement. He'd always prided himself on never showing his emotions to the outside world. Maybe he wasn't as self-contained as he thought. Or maybe Charlotte was extra-observant when it came to people's body language. He'd read somewhere that hairdressers had to be good counsellors and therapists as well. They spent as much time talking to their clients as he did.

'So is this why you've come out here to visit your sister?' she went on. 'Because she's the only one who understands how you've been feeling?'

Daniel was once again taken aback at the accuracy of Charlotte's observation. He wasn't used to being read so well.

'Partially,' he replied. 'But I also had the urge to come home for a while. I've lived in LA for many years, but I always think of Sydney as home. There's no place like it,' he said as he glanced around.

Their table was less than ten metres from the harbour, which he was facing. To his left loomed the magnificent coat-hanger-shaped harbour bridge. To his right, the truly splendid opera house with its white sail roof and absolutely perfect setting. Right on a point that jutted out into the harbour.

'I fully agree,' she said. 'I know exactly what you mean about that urge to come home. I lived overseas for years, but in the end all I wanted to do was come home to Australia.'

When she picked up her coffee he did likewise, sipping and soaking in some of the sunshine whilst he admired the beautiful city he had been born in.

'Daniel…'

'Yes?' He put down his cup and looked over at her.

'I want to thank you. For everything. Regardless of your motives. You were wonderful with my parents at lunch-time. And very agreeable about the food. I know it was pretty simple fare.'

'I enjoyed it immensely.'

'Oh, come, now. A big-shot divorce lawyer from the Hollywood hills would be used to the best of wine and food, *and* the most sophisticated of company.'

Used to them. And bored silly with them. 'I much prefer the company I had today. And the company I'll have tomorrow.'

'What about after that, Daniel? I mean…you're going back to the States in a fortnight, aren't you?'

'That's my plan,' Daniel said. 'Meanwhile, I thought you might like some company on that honeymoon you've already paid for. The one up at the Hunter Valley.'

Her eyes widened. 'Did I tell you about that?'

'You certainly did.'

'Good old blabbermouth me.'

'So how about it?'

She stared at him, her expressive eyes betraying her. She wanted him to come with her. He could *feel* it.

'I don't think so, Daniel,' she replied, stunning him. 'As much as I find you a very attractive man, I don't want to risk becoming emotionally involved with you. You've made your position on marriage quite clear so to spend more time with you would be foolish. The reason I was marrying Gary was because he said he wanted what I wanted. Marriage. And children. I'm thirty-three years old. I haven't got enough time to waste on another man who won't give me what I want. I'll spend tomorrow night with you. But come the following morning, that will be it for us.'

Her stance both impressed and sobered Daniel. All his adult life, it had been him laying down the law about what he wanted and didn't want in a relationship. He'd finally come across a woman who was capable of telling him what *she* wanted, right from the start. Usually, in the beginning, his girlfriends were more than willing to go along with his sex-only demands, perhaps because they hoped to trap him into more.

Charlotte was willing to give him one night. But only that one night. After that, she was sending him off with a flea in his ear.

Wow. What a woman. The kind of woman a man would be crazy not to want for much more than one night. The urge to pull her into his arms and tell her he was already emotionally involved was incredibly strong.

But he stopped himself. Such an action would be counter-productive at this stage.

Past hurts had made Charlotte very determined. And extremely wary. If he told her he just might have changed his mind about lots of things since meeting her, she would think he was lying; conning her so that he could have his wicked way with her for more than a night.

He had to pretend to go along with her wishes.

But as much as she was determined to resist him, he was determined to have her.

For a lot longer than their 'wedding' night. Not marriage, of course. Daniel would never embrace that unrealistic and unreliable institution.

But marriage was not the only alternative for a future relationship.

'Fair enough,' he said, pleased to see she looked disappointed by his easy agreement. 'So what are you going to tell your family about us?'

'That's my problem. I'll drive you back to your sister's place the morning after the wedding, then go up to the Hunter Valley on my own. That should give me time enough to decide when and how to tell my parents that our marriage didn't work out.'

'Speaking of our marriage,' Daniel said, 'perhaps you'd better fill me in on all the details about tomorrow. Times, places, et cetera. And then, if you don't mind, could you give me a lift back to Beth's house? It might be easier if we explained what we're going to do tomorrow together.'

'Oh, no, do I have to?'

Daniel wasn't worried. He knew Beth was going to like Charlotte. A lot.

'Yes, Charlotte,' he said firmly. 'You have to.'

CHAPTER SEVEN

'ARE you absolutely sure about this, Charlotte?' Louise asked. 'It'll be too late afterwards.'

Charlotte, who was sitting on one of their wooden kitchen chairs with a plastic cape around her shoulders, took a moment to snap out of her daydreaming. For a split-second, she thought Louise was talking about her decision to go through with the fake wedding later that day. But then she realised Louise was giving her one last chance to back out of her decision to get rid of her blonde hair.

'Absolutely,' she said.

Changing her hair was one thing she *was* sure about. Her going through with the fake wedding— whilst impossible to back out of now—was still causing her concern.

She should have told her parents the truth straight away. She could see that now. Pretending to marry Daniel, then spending the night in the bridal suite as his bride, was asking for trouble.

The man was dynamite. And she…she was a silly fool.

Already she could feel herself being drawn into his web, into wanting more than one night with him. Who knew how she'd feel tomorrow morning if he was as good in bed as she suspected he was going to be?

And maybe he was bargaining on that. He'd been all too ready to agree to her saying he couldn't come on the honeymoon with her. She wouldn't mind betting he still hoped to persuade her otherwise. *She* could only hope that when the time came, she would have the courage—and the character—to say no to him.

'Be it on your head, then,' Louise said blithely, and began applying the deep-walnut-brown colour.

'Well, it will be, won't it? On my head, that is.'

'Very funny.'

'Come, now, Louise, you always said my being blonde was not my best look. Underneath, I agreed with you. Now that I don't have to please Gary any more, I can't wait to go back to being a brunette.'

'So who are you trying to please this time? Not this Daniel, I hope. You haven't fallen for him, have you?'

Charlotte should not have hesitated in answering.

'Oh, you have!'

'No, no, I haven't,' she denied. 'But he's the sort of man a girl could easily fall for. You haven't met him, Louise. Wait till you do. Then you'll understand. He had Mum and Dad eating out of his hand in no time flat. It was almost embarrassing. But impressive.'

'Sounds like another empty charmer to me. Like Gary. And Dwayne. They both had the gift of the gab. You always go for the guys with the silver tongues.'

'He's nothing like Gary or Dwayne,' Charlotte said. He was far more dangerous than either of them.

Charlotte could see now that neither Gary nor Dwayne had *meant* to betray her. They'd just been weak.

There was nothing remotely weak about Daniel.

'You'll see when you meet him,' she repeated.

'I can't wait. Neither can Brad.'

'I wish you hadn't told Brad the truth.'

'You didn't really expect me not to tell him, did you? He has to get dressed with this guy at the hotel today and hold his hand till you show up and pretend to marry him. Brad can smell a rat a mile away. He'd have known something was up.'

'I suppose so.'

'Don't worry. He really liked the sound of Daniel. Brad admires the go-getters in this world.'

Charlotte shivered inside. The last thing she needed to hear today was how much of a go-getter Daniel was. She was trying not to think too much about him at all. She had a wedding to prepare for and get through.

Which rather made a mockery of her decision to revert to being a brunette. If she was strictly honest with herself, Charlotte had to confess she wanted to blow Daniel away today with how she looked.

Her so-called pride had given way to sheer vanity. She would pay the price, she knew, if he fancied her even more as a brunette. But she simply couldn't resist the temptation to eliminate the one thing about her he probably liked the least.

Her fake blonde hair.

'You are going to look fab with this colour hair,' Louise said. 'Blonde hair was so not you. Daniel is going to flip when he sees you, especially wearing that sexy wedding dress. Who knows? Maybe he'll fall in love with you and the next thing you know, you'll be having a real wedding.'

'Dream on, Louise. He's a divorce lawyer with a dad who's been married five times. Daniel's dead against marriage, except when it gets him into the pants of the bride.'

'Charlotte! You're sounding as cynical as I do.'

'You get that way eventually.'

'True. But I hate to see you like that. I always liked your sweet, country-girl optimism.'

'Huh. That's just a nice way of saying I was naive and stupid. Well, I don't intend being naive and stupid any longer. I'm going to spend one night with Daniel, just to see if he's as hot in bed as he looks, and the next day I'm off.'

'You're not taking him on the honeymoon with you?'

'Absolutely not.'

'But why not? I bet he'd go.'

'I'm sure he would. But I can't use men like you do, Louise. I'm not cut out for it. I'd fall in love and have my heart broken all over again.'

'You're right. You would.'

Both girls fell silent for a while.

'You really think I use men?' Louise asked finally.

Charlotte sighed. She loved Louise. The girl had been a good friend to her. But she was awfully hard on the opposite sex. She believed none of them were capable of true love, only true lust, which Louise estimated had about a six-month shelf-life. She and Brad had been together for just on six months.

'Brad really loves you, Louise.'

Louise snorted. 'I know what Brad loves. That's why I'm dating him. Man, but that guy is good in bed. And he can go all night.'

'*Really? All* night?'

'He's awesome,' Louise said with feeling in her voice.

'If Daniel doesn't work out, maybe you could lend me Brad for a night,' Charlotte quipped.

'Over my dead body, girl.'

'See? You love him,' Charlotte said, and glanced up at her friend. 'It's not just sex.'

Louise stopped painting on the colour for a second. 'Yeah. I probably do. But I don't intend telling him that. Not yet, anyway. I want to see what he does after the gloss wears off. Which should be any day now. But back to you, lovey dovey. Why don't I fix you up with one of Brad's mates in a week or two? He's got plenty.'

Charlotte didn't doubt it. Brad was a very outgoing guy with loads of energy and a great sense of humour.

'I don't think so, Louise. I think I'll just forget about dating for a while.'

'Don't leave it too long. You know what they say. When you fall off a horse, you should get right back on again.'

Charlotte didn't respond to this advice. She suspected that Daniel would be the straw that broke her back where men were concerned. She sat there in silence, fiddling with the diamond and sapphire engagement ring Gary had given her, and which she was forced to keep wearing, at least till after the wedding.

The wedding...

A wave of depression suddenly swamped her as she realised the utter futility of today. And tonight. Any silly hope that she was going to suddenly blossom seemed ludicrous. Blonde or brunette, she was the same girl who'd been consistently dumped and cheated on by her boyfriends in the past. The same clueless Charlotte.

By tomorrow morning, Daniel would be relieved that he wasn't coming on the honeymoon with her. He'd probably be bolting for the bridal-suite door before breakfast, only too happy to leave her to her misery.

Charlotte's sucked-in sobs had Louise dropping the brush back into the basin and running round to kneel in front of her friend.

The sight of her best friend's flooded eyes brought a huge lump to her throat. Truly, she could be such a fool at times. She should have anticipated how fragile Charlotte would be this morning.

'There there,' she said softly. 'I'd give you a hug, except I'd end up with a walnut-coloured face. You don't want your chief bridesmaid looking like she bought a cheap tanning product, do you?'

A watery smile broke through Charlotte's tears. 'I guess not.'

'Look, I know today is going to be hard for you,

Charlotte, but just keep remembering why you're doing it,' she said encouragingly. 'You said you couldn't bear to hurt your folks. Nothing else matters today, does it? Not really.'

'You're right,' Charlotte returned, dashing her tears away with her hands. 'I'm being pathetic. And so typically female. Don't worry, Louise. I'll be fine. Get back to my hair. I want to be the most beautiful bride I can be today. I want my mum and dad to feel nothing but pride.'

'Atta girl!' Louise said, thinking privately that that wouldn't be too hard.

Dear Daniel was in for one big surprise when he saw Charlotte. He might have lusted after her yesterday. But today, the bride was going to lift the groom's desire to another level entirely!

CHAPTER EIGHT

'So, GARY, is this the first time you've been married?'

Daniel stopped tying his bow-tie to give his supposed best man a thoughtful glance.

Brad was in his mid-twenties, a tall, lean guy with sandy hair and a cheeky grin. A real-estate assessor, he'd been dating Charlotte's best friend for about six months, despite being a decade younger. He seemed intelligent, and highly amused by something. It didn't take a genius to figure out what.

'OK, *Brad*,' Daniel returned, 'let's cut the crap. You obviously know the real deal here, so you can forget calling me Gary. In private, that is. My name is Daniel,' he said, extending his hand for the second time. 'Daniel Bannister.'

Brad grinned as he shook it. 'Great to know you, Dan. Sorry about the charade. I can never resist a laugh. But for what it's worth, I think what you're doing for Charlotte is real neat. She's a great girl. You sure you don't want to marry her for real?'

Daniel smiled. 'Apart from the legalities which could not be overcome at such short notice, I don't think that would be a very sensible thing to do. I only met Charlotte yesterday,' he finished, and went back to tying his tie.

'So what? I knew within minutes of meeting Lou

that she was the girl for me. What a hot babe! Trouble is she's a tough cookie. Been burnt a few times. But I'm going to marry her one day, no question about it.'

'Have you asked her?'

'Sure. The very first week. Lou laughed so hard and for so long that I decided not to ask again for a while. She says younger guys are good for only one thing and it's not marriage.' He grinned again. 'But I'm making headway. We sometimes spend time together out of bed now.'

Daniel had to laugh. But the word 'bed' propelled his mind to tonight. A lot rested on tonight. Frankly, he'd never felt such sexual pressure. Today was proving to be much more stressful than he had anticipated.

'To answer your first question,' he said, undoing his slightly lopsided tie and starting again, 'no, I've never been married before.'

'So you're on the market, eh, Dan?'

'I'm a bachelor, yes.'

'How old are you, exactly?'

'Thirty-six.'

'Girlfriend back home?'

'Not at the moment.'

'Lou says you're a lawyer. A well-heeled one by the look of you.'

'I'm comfortably off.'

Rather an understatement of his financial status.

'Comfortably off' would have been an accurate description of Daniel's wealth prior to his investing in a movie four years earlier. At the time, one of his female clients—a middle-aged actress—had just been dumped by her producer husband. When she showed him this script she'd bought and which she claimed would revitalise her career, Daniel had read it more out of sympathy than anything, but found himself totally engrossed. He'd invested as much as he could find in it, and talked all his partners into putting up the rest.

The independently made thriller had gone on to be a huge hit and the money had been rolling in ever since.

'I've made a few wise investments over the years,' he added.

Brad chuckled. 'You're a cool dude, aren't you? What a pity you don't want to marry our Charlotte for real. You'd make her a good husband, I reckon. Not that Lou agrees. She thinks you're only interested in getting into Charlotte's pants.'

'What?' Daniel whirled round, his abrupt action reefing his tie back undone.

Brad shrugged. 'That's Lou for you. If she can believe the worst of a bloke, she will. Personally, I can't see anything wrong with your wanting to get Charlotte into bed. That girl's a looker all right. And she could do with being laid by a guy who knows how.'

Daniel tried not to look too shocked. But shocked he was. 'I don't think we should be discussing Charlotte's private life, do you?' he said somewhat stiffly.

Brad was taken aback by the reproof. 'Oh. Er— yeah. Right. If you say so. It's just that Lou said you were going to spend the night with her in some fancy honeymoon suite here in the hotel so I thought I'd better warn you up front.'

'Right. Thanks.'

'No sweat.'

Daniel went back to tying his bow-tie, Brad's astonishing news revolving in his mind. Who would have imagined that the girl who'd kissed him so passionately was so sexually inexperienced. Perhaps she just hadn't had the right partner yet.

He tried tying his bow-tie for the third time but it ended up crooked again.

'You're not too good at that, are you?' Brad said.

Daniel's sigh carried frustration. 'Normally I am.'

'Maybe you're more nervous than you look.'

'What's there to be nervous about?' he retorted, his clumsiness having irritated him. 'This is just pretend.'

'The speeches aren't pretend, mate.'

'Speeches? You mean, I have to give a *speech*?'

'Yep. You're the groom. Haven't you been to any weddings?'

'I avoid them.' Difficult to share in the joy of a wedding when you were a divorce lawyer, and when your father had been married five times. He would have happily gone to Beth's wedding, but Beth and her husband had eloped.

'You must have seen movies with weddings in them,' Brad said with a touch of exasperation in his voice. '*My Best Friend's Wedding. Four Weddings and a Funeral.* There was a cracker of a speech in that flick. But I don't think it was the groom's speech,' Brad said, stroking his chin. 'It was the best man's. That's me. I have to give a speech about you. *You* have to give a speech about the bride. Nothing funny. Mushy stuff. Like how you felt when you first met her. What you think of her family. How much you love her. Stuff like that.'

Daniel grimaced. This was going to be more difficult than he'd imagined. Speeches were his stock in trade, but this was totally different from addressing a jury.

'Take some advice from an old hand at this kind of speech,' Brad said, stepping forward and doing Daniel's bow-tie for him. 'Kiss is the answer.'

Daniel blinked. 'Huh?'

'Don't you know that saying in America? Kiss? K I S S. Keep it simple, stupid. Just say how gorgeous she is, how much you love her, and how you would go to the ends of the earth for her. Which you have,' Brad added with a guffaw. 'Can't go much farther than Australia, mate. Unless you want to live with the penguins down in Antarctica. Right! Your tie's done. You're all set.'

'Thanks,' Daniel said before scooping in a steadying breath and telling himself he could handle this.

A glance at his watch revealed that it was thirteen minutes to four. The wedding was scheduled for four. Time to get out there. But first of all, he checked the breast pocket of his jacket for something. Yes. It was there.

'Have you got the rings?' he asked the best man.

Brad patted his jacket pocket. 'Yep. Both there,

safe as houses. I've done this before, mate.
Trust me.'

Daniel nodded. 'I can see that. You've been a
great help. To be honest, I don't know what I'd have
done without you.' His tie would have been crooked
for one.

Brad looked chuffed at the compliment. 'You
know, for an American lawyer, you're OK. I thought
you were all supposed to be bastards.'

Daniel laughed. 'Don't believe everything you see
on television.'

'I was thinking of Gary.'

'Yes, well, the Garys of this world are everywhere,' he pointed out. 'Not just in America. And
not just in the legal profession. But for your information, I'm not American, despite the accent. I was
born here in Sydney. Went to school here, too.'

'Well, stone the crows! Now I know why I like
you so much.'

Daniel smiled. 'The feelings are mutual. Shall we
go?'

Both men turned as one and headed for the door.

Daniel had checked out the setting for the wedding
ceremony with Vince earlier in the day, Vince having
agreed last night to act as celebrant. It was to be held
on the ground floor of the hotel, in a conservatory
that was in keeping with the old-fashioned and very
romantic decor of the Regency Royale.

There was a huge domed glass ceiling, reminiscent
of bygone eras, plus a circular flagstone floor fringed
by lots of exotic flowering plants and palms. All the

walls of the hexagonal structure were made of glass, except for one section opposite the entrance. It looked as if it was made of rock, and a constant stream of water ran down the façade to an ornamental pool at the base.

The wedding ceremony was to take place in front of this pool and waterfall.

When Daniel had been shown the conservatory this morning, the flagstone floor had been dotted with black wrought-iron furniture. The conservatory was usually used as a beer garden. He'd been assured the furniture would all be cleared away and replaced by clean white chairs, neatly arranged in two curved rows on each side of the circular floor to give all the guests a perfect view. A strip of rich red carpet would bisect these rows, ending in a T shape in front of the waterfall. An elegantly carved wooden podium would be provided for the celebrant to stand behind, as well as a white linen-covered table for the signing of the marriage documents.

'Wow!' Brad exclaimed as they walked through the entrance to the conservatory.

Daniel was equally surprised. The transformation in the conservatory was much more than had been described to him that morning. They had said nothing of the masses of added flowers. Or the wonderful music. Or the two splendidly uniformed men standing to attention on each side of the entrance, like footmen of old.

But it was the atmosphere that struck Daniel the most, the excited energy that was coming from the well-dressed guests, most of whom were already seated. At Daniel's appearance on the red carpet, all heads had jerked up and around, everyone either smiling or staring at him.

Of course, Daniel didn't know a single face amongst them, except Charlotte's mother. Betty—dressed in pink—was beaming over at him. Beaming and waving a gloved hand.

A banging sound behind him made Daniel whirl round. The two uniformed attendants had shut the doors, which, Daniel noticed for the first time, were not clear glass but heavily stained. Impossible to see through them.

'That's so you don't see the bride till the time is right,' Brad explained. 'Brides like to make an entrance.'

'I see,' Daniel bit out, wishing now that he'd thought to have a couple of glasses of something intoxicating and soothing. He hadn't appreciated till this moment just how much of an ordeal this would be.

'This way, mate,' Brad said with a wry smile, and gave Daniel a nudge.

They proceeded along the red carpet towards the spot where Vince was waiting for them, looking suitably dignified and older than his thirty-seven years in a dark grey suit with a crisp white shirt and muted grey tie. His dark wavy hair, which was usually on the long side and decidedly wayward, had been cut this morning to make him look less like a Bohemian and more like a marriage celebrant. They'd already planned not to act as if they knew each other, Daniel shaking Vince's hand as though they'd just met. Brad did likewise after winking slyly at both of them.

As they turned together to face the stained-glass doors, the music suddenly changed from the softly romantic number currently being piped into the room to the more robust and stirring *Wedding March*.

Charlotte, it seemed, was not going to be late.

The stained-glass doors were flung open and a hush came over the guests as necks craned to get a view of the bride.

Daniel felt his chest tighten.

But it was the bridesmaid who appeared first, walking slowly along the red carpet. Louise, he presumed.

Tall and slender, she was elegantly gowned in a strapless blue dress that draped around her bust then fell in soft Grecian folds to the floor. Her hair, which was almost as red as her bouquet, was straight and sleek, and swung around her face as she walked. Her face was equally angular, but her mouth was full and sultry. Her eyes, which were possibly set too close for real beauty, were, nevertheless, striking in their blueness. Or was it their boldness?

Daniel concluded rightly that Louise would be a handful for any man. Brad had his work cut out for him if he was to succeed in his goal to marry her.

'Wow,' Brad enthused by Daniel's side. 'See what I mean? She's hot, man.'

As she drew closer, those bold blue eyes narrowed on Daniel in an assessing fashion, making him squirm a little.

Poor Brad. This female would run rings around him.

'Mmm,' she murmured in an unnervingly droll fashion when she was close enough for him to hear. 'I see what Charlotte means.'

Daniel would have liked to ask her what *that* meant, but this was hardly the time or the place. Later, maybe. Instead, he plastered a cool smile on his face and said a soft hello.

She gave him a killer look in return, then turned a full-wattage smile Brad's way.

'You look gorgeous, lover,' she whispered to Brad, before taking her place on the other side of Daniel, leaving plenty of room for Charlotte.

Daniel's focus returned to the entrance to the conservatory, where he could see a cloud of white in the dimmer light just beyond the open doors.

The bride, waiting to make her entry.

Daniel's throat suddenly went bone-dry. He swallowed, then swallowed again. Was Charlotte as nervous as he was? Was that why she was taking so long to appear?

'What's she doing?' he whispered over to the redhead.

'Taking off the small face veil, I think. She thought it didn't look right with her new hairdo.'

The words 'new hairdo' barely registered before the cloud of white came into focus and Daniel was confronted by a Charlotte he could never have envisaged.

If his throat had been dry before, it felt like parchment now.

She wasn't just beautiful. She was devastatingly beautiful. A fairy-tale princess of a bride in a dress designed to make any husband-to-be go ga-ga.

Daniel complied with a raw rush of desire.

Like Louise's, Charlotte's gown was strapless, but, where her friend's bodice was draped, this one was smooth and tight, bolstering up Charlotte's already impressive breasts whilst constricting her waist into hand-spanning size. The skirt, by contrast, was full and frothy, brushing against her father's legs as he accompanied her down the red carpet.

But her crowning glory was her hair.

Gone was the long, straight curtain of blonde hair, replaced by soft, glossy, shoulder-length waves in a glorious dark brown that glinted red when the light hit it. The rich walnut shade was a perfect foil for the dazzling whiteness of the dress and the honey-coloured skin of her bare shoulders and arms. Framing her striking face and hair was a short but very feminine veil, which was anchored on top of her head by an exquisite tiara decorated with dia-mantés and pearls. She wore no jewellery around her elegant throat. She didn't need any.

The sight of her literally took Daniel's breath away.

He was barely aware of the camera flashes going off, or the video man off to one side filming everything. His eyes were riveted on his bride, his heart pounding in a way it hadn't pounded in his entire life.

CHAPTER NINE

A WAVE of emotional confusion swamped Charlotte as she started to walk down that red carpet on her father's arm, her eyes dropping agitatedly to the bouquet she was holding.

Was she happy or sad? Regretful or resentful? Nervous or excited?

All of those things, she realised.

Happy that her hair had turned out brilliantly. But sad that she'd spent so long as a blonde, trying to please Gary. Regretful that she was wasting so much of her dad's money today, and resentful that Gary didn't give a damn. Nervous over pretending to marry Daniel, but also appallingly excited.

All day, one overriding thought had dominated Charlotte's mind.

Tonight.

Difficult to think of anything else.

Was Daniel as excited as she was?

Her eyes lifted at last to look at him.

Her step faltered. Her heart as well.

Had there ever been a more handsome groom?

People said brides always looked beautiful in their wedding dresses, even the plain ones. But the same could be said for grooms, in Charlotte's opinion. There was something about a tuxedo which made the most of any man. It gave him stature, and styling, and sophistication.

Daniel had been handsome in a business suit and impossibly sexy in jeans. In the elegant black tuxedo he was wearing today, he was *so* handsome and sexy, it was criminal.

Just looking at him was a turn-on. Being with him was going to be incredible. She could feel it in every fibre of her being.

Her resolve not to take him with her to the Hunter Valley tomorrow immediately went a bit wobbly. If the earth moved in Daniel's arms tonight, how could she possibly give him up after just one night?

But if she prolonged their affair, wouldn't that make losing him later on all the more terrible? And wasn't she just making the same mistake again, going from one relationship disaster to another, this time in a shockingly short space of time? After Dwayne it had at least been a few weeks before she met Gary. It had been less than two days since Gary had jilted her.

'Are you all right, love?'

Charlotte's head turned slowly to find her father frowning at her.

It was a defining moment for Charlotte, a moment when she realised she was sick and tired of fighting her feelings for Daniel.

She wanted to be with him. OK, so they might only have a few days together. But those few days would probably be better than a lifetime with another man.

'Yes, Dad,' she said, resigning herself to the fact

she was setting herself up for some serious heart-break this time. But what she felt was too powerful to ignore.

'I'm fine,' she added. And forced a smile to her mouth.

Her smile reassured Daniel. Till he saw her eyes.

There was sadness in her eyes.

Was she wishing it were Gary standing here, wait-ing to marry her?

Surely not. She didn't love Gary any more than Gary had loved her.

Daniel supposed *that* might be what was making her sad, her having been so mistaken, not only about Gary's feelings but also her own. No one liked to feel a fool.

Did Charlotte feel a fool?

He hoped not. Because she was far from foolish. She was sweet and brave and loving, and that stupid bloody Gary didn't deserve her. As for that Dwayne guy… Daniel would have liked to punch his lights out, the miserable jerk.

Still, Charlotte was better off without either of those two. Hell, they couldn't even make her happy in bed! The least a man could do was make his woman happy in bed.

He smiled back at her as she approached, deter-mined that he wouldn't let her down. Tonight could not come quickly enough.

'You look so beautiful,' he whispered when her father handed her over to him.

Her blue eyes sparkled this time. 'Thank you. So do you.'

Vince cleared his throat, bringing their attention back to the moment at hand.

'We are gathered here today,' he started, his having decided on a very traditional ceremony, chiefly because that was the only one he'd been able to find a copy of last night, 'to celebrate the marriage of...'

Daniel's mind drifted away from the words to concentrate on Charlotte. She was wearing more make-up today. But her glorious dark hair and the glamorous white wedding dress demanded it. With blue eye-shadow and black eye-liner, her eyes looked so big and blue. And that red gloss on her mouth made Daniel long to kiss her.

When his eyes dropped to her cleavage, he had some difficulty keeping his thoughts from straying to her beautiful breasts and the many ways in which he wanted to make love to her tonight.

Daniel determined to make it impossible for her to send him on his way tomorrow. He might not be good marriage material but he was a good lover.

He was working out his sexual strategy when he heard Vince ask who gave this woman in marriage.

Her father answered, 'I do,' proudly and then the ceremony began in earnest.

Daniel winced over being called Gary Cantrell, but swallowed his pride and said 'I do' at the right moment. Charlotte made them all suffer with a heart-stopping hesitation before *she* said 'I do'. At least she didn't have to promise to obey.

The exchange of rings carried more tension,

mainly because his was a tight fit. How was he ever going to get the darned thing off afterwards?

Daniel breathed a sigh of relief when they got to the 'I now pronounce you man and wife' part. The worst was over. Now he got to kiss the bride.

They were already facing each other, with Charlotte gazing up into his eyes with an expression Daniel found extremely flattering. No, she certainly hadn't loved Gary.

A sudden panic zoomed into her face. She didn't want him to kiss her, that much was evident.

Daniel felt put out, till he realised she might be worried he was going to kiss her as he had kissed her yesterday in the hotel lobby. That had been some kiss!

He decided he could wait till he had her behind closed doors before he unleashed his still smouldering passion. Though damn it all, controlling himself once his lips were on hers was not going to be easy.

Steeling himself, he took her face gently between his hands and gave her the softest, sweetest kiss on the mouth. No pressure. No pushing open her lips. Daniel suspected embarrassing things might happen if he did that.

But he wanted to. Hell, he wanted to desperately.

The reception loomed ahead as a far bigger trial than this wedding, because it was longer. Hours, maybe. But there was no getting out of it.

Meanwhile, he would have had to be careful not to let his frustration show. And not to drink. He had to be stone-cold sober to perform as he wanted to perform tonight.

'Love the hair,' he complimented after his mouth lifted. '*And* the dress.'

He could have added *love what's in it*, but he didn't, of course. That would have been crass. And Daniel was not crass.

Aroused, but not crass.

She stared up into his eyes with the oddest expression. Kind of dazed.

'Better than blonde?' she asked with a charming tilt of her head.

'Much,' he said. 'You made a beautiful blonde, but you're a ravishing brunette.' He certainly wanted to ravish her. Right now.

She smiled. A happy smile. No, a *dazzling* smile.

Daniel stifled a groan and managed to smile back. 'I've always been partial to brunettes,' he said truthfully.

Vince stopped any further conversation with a touch to Daniel's elbow. He led them over to the table to sign the pretend papers, which they did, along with Brad and Louise. Cameras continued to flash. The video rolled on. Daniel murmured a discreet 'thank you' to Vince, who said he would be going straight home to tell Beth all about it.

Beth, it had been obvious last night, thought this whole pretend wedding thing was *so* romantic. There again, Beth had always been an incurable romantic.

'Smile, please,' the photographer ordered. 'The groom! *Smile*, please.'

Daniel smiled.

CHAPTER TEN

'EXCUSE me a moment, please, Charlotte,' Daniel said, and pushed back his chair.

Charlotte's eyes followed him as he stood up and walked to the table where her father was seated. There was an empty chair next to her dad, her mother having temporarily vacated it.

The reception had been in full swing for over an hour, with the entrée and the main meal having been served. Charlotte had chosen the menu herself, but hadn't really enjoyed any of the food. In fact, she'd just picked at it.

From the moment Daniel had said she was ravishing, her hunger hadn't been for food.

Her eyes were still glued to him when he suddenly glanced back over his shoulder at her. Embarrassed at being caught staring, she pulled her eyes away and picked up her glass. She might not have eaten much but she'd been downing the wine. Chardonnay. Her favourite.

'See what I told you would happen?' Louise whispered to Charlotte. 'He can't take his eyes off you.'

'More like the other way around. I…I've never wanted a man like I do him. I think I will take him away on my honeymoon holiday after all.'

Louise gave a softly knowing laugh. 'Aah, so you

know now what I feel when I'm with Brad. Nothing like a bit of good old-fashioned lust, is there?'

'Lust…' Charlotte frowned. 'How can I be sure that's all this is?'

'What else, at this early stage? Goodness, don't go thinking what you feel is *love*, girl. I have to admit, if I wasn't so taken with Brad, I might bat my eyelashes in Daniel's direction as well.'

'Did I hear someone mention my name?' Brad said from his seat on the other side of Daniel's vacant one.

Louise rolled her eyes. 'Amazing how his ears always prick up every time he hears his name. That's men for you. Yes, Brad, we were both talking about you and how yummy you look in your tux.'

'I was thinking the same about you, babe.'

'What, how good I'd look in your tux?'

Brad laughed. 'You're a crack-up, Lou. You really are. Aah, here's Dan back again. Ready for your speech, mate? We're on soon.'

'Ready as I'll ever be,' Daniel replied as he sat down. 'Your dad tells me he's up first, Charlotte.'

'What were you talking to him about?' she asked, her mind still pondering Louise's assertion that what she felt for Daniel was just lust.

'Nothing for you to worry about.'

The MC's announcement that the father of the bride was going to speak had Charlotte falling silent, but her head was still spinning. She supposed Louise was probably right. Louise knew what she was talking about where lust was concerned, whereas Charlotte was a right novice.

But even if it was just lust stirring her, Charlotte still worried that several days spent with Daniel could make her feelings for him deepen. Louise was made of tougher stuff than she was. She didn't appreciate the risk.

But Charlotte couldn't see herself resisting the temptation. Not unless tonight was a disaster.

Her father's tapping the microphone cut into her thoughts, bringing her back to the present. The speeches. It was not a moment she'd been looking forward to.

'I'm not one for giving speeches, as you probably all know,' her father began. 'I'm a farmer and farmers are at their best with their backsides on a tractor and their mouths shut.'

Everyone laughed. Everyone except Charlotte. She was too aware of Daniel sitting next to her, too strung up with nerves.

'We're best left in the country, too. But I'm not just a farmer. I'm a father, too. And a father will do anything for a daughter. So here I am in this fancy city hotel, eating fancy food and drinking fancy wine. But I can tell you right now that I've never had a happier day in all my life.'

Charlotte jumped in her seat when Daniel suddenly picked up her hand and squeezed it. 'Do try to look a little happier,' he whispered. 'You're supposed to be wildly in love with me. Smile a bit more.'

Somehow she found another smile, though her mouth was beginning to ache with all the smiling.

'Yes, that's it,' he said, giving her hand another squeeze. 'Not long to go now. Hang in there.'

'Of course, we all know that Charlotte has not followed the usual path of a country girl,' her dad continued. 'There were moments where I thought I would never see her as she is today. As a bride. And for that I have to thank Gary. I only had to know my future son-in-law for ten seconds before I understood why our Charlotte had fallen head over heels with a man I thought she hardly knew. As for Gary…have you ever seen a man so handsome, or so much in love?'

Everyone clapped and cheered. Charlotte wanted to cry.

'They say you can tell a man by his actions more than his words. Gary told me to keep this a secret but I want to tell you that just now, my new son-in-law is going to pay for this wedding.'

More clapping and cheering.

Charlotte, however, was speechless.

'Oh-oh,' Daniel said out of the corner of his mouth. 'You don't look pleased. I thought you'd be happy that your father wouldn't be out of pocket.'

'But it wasn't your place! I would have paid him back after I told him we'd separated. Every single cent.'

'Hey, hush up, you two,' Brad said.

They hushed up, leaving Charlotte to simmer in silence. If he'd been her real groom, it would have been an incredibly generous gesture. As it was, she suspected it was more a corrupting gesture, a type of advance payment on services to be rendered.

The thought infuriated her. But it also flattered her. Right from the start, Daniel's pursuit had been incredibly aggressive. Clearly, he would stop at nothing to have her.

What woman wouldn't thrill to a man being so taken by her charms? What she had to keep remembering, however, was that it was just a sexual interest. Wealthy playboys like Daniel didn't want women for anything else. They might pretend to value other things in their partners, but the bottom line was sex. Plus the challenge of the chase. Charlotte suspected that once she'd capitulated and he'd had her a few times, Daniel's passion would begin to wane.

His own sister had warned her that his girlfriends came and went.

Charlotte tried to stay angry with her logical, if somewhat cynical, thoughts. But it was impossible. She just felt more and more excited. Louise was right. This was just lust on her part. She couldn't think about anything else.

Her father spoke for another couple of minutes, giving them some advice over the tolerance necessary for a happy marriage then wishing them all the happiness in the world before offering the official toast to the bride and groom.

Charlotte plastered a plastic smile on her face and willed for the reception to be over. She couldn't wait to be alone with Daniel, and to have him kiss her once more. Not the way he'd kissed her after the ceremony. The way he'd kissed her in the lobby yesterday.

After her father sat down, it was Brad's turn to speak. Charlotte winced as he stood up. Lord knew what he was going to say. Something embarrassing, that was for sure.

'My job as best man today,' he began, 'is a little awkward. A best man is usually the groom's best mate, or his big brother. Someone who has known him for yonks. But I only met this good-looking fella a couple of hours ago. The other times I've been best man at a wedding, it's been dead easy to tell some naughty stories about what the groom has been up to over the years. I have those kind of mates,' he added, grinning. 'But I can't do that with Gary here. But you know what? I reckon there *are* no naughty stories in Gary's past. Pete said he knew straight away what kind of bloke was marrying his daughter. I felt the same way. This man here,' he said, resting a hand on Daniel's shoulder, 'is one of the good guys. True blue, in our Aussie language. I told him when we were getting dressed that he'd made a fantastic husband for our beautiful bride here and I meant it. By the way, she is beautiful, don't you agree?'

More clapping and cheering. Charlotte groaned. Talk about torment!

'But it's not my job to gush over the bride. That's Gary's. My job is to gush over the bridesmaid. Not a hard job to do, considering we're an item,' he added with a wink Louise's way. 'I might be biased but I've never seen a better-looking bridesmaid. And that dress... Wow, babe. You should wear blue more often. Although I'd really like to see you in white.'

More clapping and cheering and shouts of, 'Hear! hear!'

Louise blushed furiously, which was a first for Louise.

Brad proposed the toast to Louise, Charlotte grateful for another swallow of the delicious champagne.

Daniel, she noticed, barely sipped his.

She didn't look up at him when he stood up, but kept her eyes focused on the back part of the room.

'Brad might have been to a good few weddings,' were his opening words. 'But strangely, I've never been to one. So forgive me if my speech doesn't follow the norm. Firstly, I want to thank my best man for doing such a sterling job today, and the lovely Louise for all the help and friendship she has given Charlotte. I also want to thank the Gales for the wonderful way they have welcomed me into their family. I can honestly say that I have never met their like before. Charlotte is very fortunate to have such exceptionally loving parents. Very fortunate indeed.'

Charlotte resisted the temptation to roll her eyes, but heavens to Betsy, did he have to lay it on that thick? Clearly, he was relishing the role of man of the moment. Every single person in the room was smiling at him. Of course, all her relatives already thought he was the ant's pants because he was taking troublesome Charlotte off the single shelf. If they only knew!

She sighed, then made the mistake of glancing up at Daniel.

When he smiled back down at her, she found she could not look away. Her gaze remained locked to his, her insides dissolving. She was helpless when he smiled at her like that. Helpless and hopeless.

'What can I say about Charlotte?' he said quietly, his eyes caressing hers. 'She *is* beautiful, there is no doubt about that. But she is beautiful on the inside as well as the outside. That might sound clichéd but with Charlotte, nothing is clichéd. She is a remarkable woman and any man would be lucky to have her as his wife. No, not lucky. Privileged. My life hasn't been the same since the first moment we met. Actually, Brad was wrong when he said there were no naughty stories to be told about me. There have been. Quite a few. But no longer. I'm a changed man. Charlotte has changed me.'

At last he looked away from her, and all the breath suddenly rushed out of her lungs from where she'd been holding it.

Louise leant close to her right ear. 'If I didn't know better, I'd think he meant all that.'

Charlotte almost laughed. She wished.

He was a good actor, that was all. A polished performer. He'd be dynamite in the courtroom.

Dynamite in the bedroom, too, an insidious voice inserted.

'I've been told I have to propose a toast to my bride. So raise your glasses, everyone. To my lovely Charlotte…' And he looked down at her again.

Daniel was taken aback by the sarcastic light that glittered in Charlotte's eyes as he drank to her.

What on earth was going on in that girl's head?

He'd expected her to be a bit unhappy today.

Maybe even bitter. But with Gary, not him. He was trying to be a good guy, as Brad had said.

She hadn't liked him paying for the wedding. Pride, he supposed. Charlotte was proud.

Well, that was too bad because he'd liked giving the Gales that money. He could well afford it and it had made both of them very happy. If Charlotte chose not to see it in that light, then that was her problem.

Frankly, he was getting just a tad irritated with her. She should have been grateful for all he'd done, not looking daggers at him.

When he sat back down, Brad gave him a poke in the ribs. 'You have to go cut the cake now.'

Daniel sighed. Would this ever end?

They stood up together with Daniel putting his hand on Charlotte's elbow as they made their way round to the table that housed the three-tiered wedding cake. More smiles. More photographs.

'And now,' the MC boomed, 'the bride and groom will take the floor for the bridal waltz.'

Daniel winced. He'd actually heard of the bridal waltz and always thought it sounded schmaltzy. Suddenly, it seemed hazardous as well. He would have to take Charlotte in his arms and hold her close, and God only knew what would happen after that.

Daniel hesitated, despite the music having started up.

'Surely you know how to dance,' his bride said, again with that caustic gleam in her eye.

Right. He'd had enough of this.

With no further ado, he swept her into his arms

and onto the dance floor, twirling her round with elegant ease.

His fears over dancing with Charlotte, however, proved correct. No sooner had one hand been clamped to the small of her back and the other curled round her hot little hand than he felt the none too subtle stirrings of his flesh.

Thank goodness for the bridal gown, with its huge skirt and masses of petticoats. No way would Charlotte be able to feel a thing, he soon realised, smiling ruefully as he danced on, masochistically enjoying his arousal.

'You're looking very pleased with yourself,' she tossed at him.

'I'll be a lot more pleased when this reception is over,' he replied, and pulled her just a little closer.

That shut her up.

'Did you give the porter your overnight bag like we arranged?' he asked, his mind now solidly on the aftermath of this reception.

'Yes,' she replied a bit breathlessly.

'Good.' Daniel didn't want anything going wrong tonight. He had everything planned, and arranged.

'Er—which one of the bridal suites did you book?' she asked.

There'd only been the one available. The most expensive one.

'The Arabian Nights suite,' he replied, and listened, with a surge of triumph, as she gasped.

CHAPTER ELEVEN

CHARLOTTE gasped, then gulped. The Arabian Nights suite!

Oh…my…God…

Somehow Charlotte got through the bridal waltz, and the rest of the reception. She smiled at all her relatives when they came up to congratulate her and thanked them for their gifts, which were piled up on a huge table at the back of the reception room.

Charlotte had known not to bother with that bridal-register idea at any of the department stores where guests could order presents from a list and have them delivered to the bride's house beforehand. Country folk liked to bring their presents to the actual wedding.

Louise kept asking her if she was all right and she kept saying she was fine.

But she wasn't fine. In her head, she was already in that decadent bridal suite, in that decadent bed, gazing up at the decadent, mirrored ceiling.

Charlotte had been shown all the themed bridal suites when she'd first made enquiries here at the hotel, so she knew exactly what the Arabian Nights suite entailed. Not only was it the most expensive, but it was also the most exotic—and erotic—in decor.

By the time her mother hugged her goodbye,

brushing a tear from her eye, Charlotte's already strung-out nerves were stretched tight as a drum.

'Look after her for us, Gary,' her father said as he pumped Daniel's hand, then turned to hug his daughter.

'And you look after your husband, Charlotte,' he advised.

'I will, Dad,' she choked out.

'Now, off you go, you two, and have a great honeymoon. And don't worry about your wedding presents. Louise and Brad said they'd take them home for you and look after them. Mother and I will be taking off pretty early in the morning so this is goodbye from us for now. Give us a call after you get back from your honeymoon, OK?'

Daniel said they would.

Thankfully, there was a bank of lifts just outside the reception-room doors into which the 'honeymooners' raced to the cheers and claps of the happily intoxicated guests.

Fortunately, the lift they caught was empty. It whisked them up to the tenth floor, Charlotte only then realising she'd possibly drunk too much wine on her mostly empty stomach. She'd only managed a bite or two of the dessert, and none of the coffee and mints afterwards.

'You all right?' Daniel asked when the doors whooshed open and she stayed clasping the brass railing that ran around the lift wall at hand-height.

'I think I had a bit too much to drink.'

'I noticed you didn't eat much. Are you feeling sick?'

He looked worried, Charlotte noticed.

'I'll be all right. Just a slight dizzy spell from the lift.'

'Here. Take my arm.'

She smiled a wry smile as she did so. 'Is this you looking after me?'

He grinned. 'Absolutely. You can look after me later.'

Suddenly, Charlotte was overcome with panic. Because she knew what Daniel meant. Without a doubt, he was expecting her to be a woman of the world, experienced and confident.

'Daniel, I... There's something I have to tell you,' she said. She had to warn him; had to explain that she was not the sexy piece she seemed.

'There's nothing you have to tell me, beautiful,' he said softly, pulling her round into his arms. 'Tonight is my responsibility, not yours. You don't have to do a thing. Just lie back and enjoy.'

His words brought a rush of relief, Charlotte realising that if she'd told him she was bad—or boring—in bed, everything would have been spoilt in advance. This way, she had a chance to become the wanton woman she was in her fantasies.

'But I don't think I should kiss you just yet,' he said ruefully. 'Better we get behind closed doors first.'

A shudder rippled down her spine. 'Closed doors sounds good,' she agreed. 'Have you—er—got the passkey to the suite?'

'Right here.' And he patted his pocket.

'Did you come up to see this particular suite before you booked it?'

'No. Should I have? Is there something wrong with it?'

'Not at all,' Charlotte denied.

But he was in for a surprise. She hoped he liked it. She certainly had, despite being initially startled.

Daniel saw the gleam in her eyes and wondered what was waiting for him. Whatever it was, he was sure he would approve. Anything that pleased Charlotte this much would please him.

The Arabian Nights suite was the first one along the carpeted corridor, its name outlined in gold on the door. Shoving the plastic card into the lock, Daniel waited for the green light, turned the brass handle then pushed the rather heavy door open. The darkness inside was soon dispelled when he slid the card into the slot by the door, the lights coming on automatically.

'Good God!' he couldn't help exclaiming.

'You think it's over-the-top?' she asked, sounding disappointed by his reaction.

'No, no, it's fabulous.'

Her face beamed with more happiness than it had all night.

'Come and see the rest,' she said excitedly, taking his hand and pulling him across the black, marble-floored foyer and under a very ornate Moroccan-style archway. There, the marble gave way to thick, velvety red carpet that sank underfoot further than any carpet he'd ever encountered.

'This carpet is amazing,' he said. Just made for making love on.

And so were the sofas!

There were three of them. Low and wide and colourful, they were slightly curved, arranged around a circular, black-lacquered coffee-table on which rested a huge platter of fresh fruit, and a gilt ice bucket holding a magnum of champagne.

Beyond the sofas, curtains the colour of the water around Tahiti framed a floor-to-ceiling window that showed a panoramic view of the city skyline. There was no overhead lighting. Only lamps and wall lights. All gold. All exotic-looking.

'Look up at the ceiling,' she said.

His eyes moved up the deep blue walls to the very high ceiling above, which was draped in black silk shot with gold.

Wow. He now understood why this place had cost so much.

'Fit for a sheikh,' he remarked.

'That's the idea. It's supposed to tap into people's fantasies.'

'Do you have a sheikh fantasy?' he asked, reaching to pull her into his arms once more.

She gasped as their chests made contact. 'Only if you're the sheikh.'

He liked the sound of that.

'So tell me,' he murmured as he set about removing her tiara and veil, 'how does that fantasy go?'

Charlotte shivered at the touch of his fingers in her hair.

'You have your wicked way with me all night,'

she confessed breathlessly. 'And I love every single moment.'

'That's not fantasy, my beautiful Charlotte. That's going to be reality.' He tossed her veil and tiara onto the nearest sofa, before suddenly quirking an eyebrow at her. '*All* night?'

'See? I told you it was a fantasy.'

'No, no. I'm sure I can rise to the challenge. But I have only limited protection with me. I will have to be inventive when they run out. Do you mind inventive, beautiful Charlotte?'

'I don't think I'd mind anything with you,' she told him truthfully as her heart thundered behind her ribs.

Daniel suppressed a groan. There went his intentions to be a caring, considerate and conservative lover tonight.

Still, she clearly didn't want a caring, considerate and conservative lover tonight. She wanted the sheikh fantasy, where the dark and dangerous desert prince carried her off by force, thereby wiping away any sense of shame or guilt if she just happened to enjoy herself. She wanted him to take total responsibility for what happened here tonight. She wanted him to play the sheikh.

Fine. He could do that. Especially here, in this incredibly erotic setting. He'd already glimpsed the bedroom through another archway and it made the exotic living room look almost sedate.

'Come,' he said in a masterful tone. 'We shall retire to the boudoir.'

'Wait till you see it!'

Daniel tried not to ooh and aah.

But talk about harem territory. This was full-on.

'I'm sure honeymooners love it,' Charlotte said with a nervous little laugh.

Not just honeymooners, Daniel thought as he looked from the raised, black-lacquered four-poster bed with its filmy white curtains up to the mirrored ceiling above. Once again, the carpet underfoot was lush and thick, though this time it was green. Emerald-green. Everything else in the room, however, was black, white or silver.

'Lots of silver,' he commented. The wallpaper was silver, and so were the edges of the mirrors, and the thread running through the white satin quilt. 'I would have expected gold.'

'The bathroom has gold fittings,' she said. 'To go with the black marble, I guess.'

'They said it had a spa bath.'

'Yes, a huge one.' She flushed at the mention of the bath.

Surely not from shyness, Daniel reasoned. No woman who'd chosen the wedding dress she was wearing was shy about her body.

'Good,' he said.

Daniel decided any more delay would be counter-productive. 'I think it's time to check out that bathroom,' he said, reaching for her. 'But first, let's get you out of that dress.' And he turned her round.

CHAPTER TWELVE

CHARLOTTE sucked in sharply when his hands started work on the laces that anchored the bustier top to her body. Louise had tied them very tightly so that her waist was pulled in as far as it would go, the compression pushing her ribs in and her breasts upwards, giving her an extreme, hourglass shape.

She wore no bra. None had been needed, the top of her gown heavily boned and lined. Once Daniel got the laces undone, Charlotte knew that the top would fall from her body, leaving her naked from the waist up.

Just the thought turned her on.

She'd never been this eager to be naked before. Or to have a man's hands on her body.

'Aah, now I get it,' Daniel said as the bodice went slack around her. 'The top's separate from the skirt.'

The freeing of her breasts from the skin-tight constriction brought with it a wave of melting heat. When he removed the top right away from her body, she swayed.

'Hey!' he said softly, his arms sliding around her just underneath her breasts. 'Don't go fainting on me.'

Her answer was a soft moan, her eyes fluttering shut as she leant back against him in blissful surrender.

When his hands moved upwards to cup her breasts she almost cried out, her nipples stabbing at the centre of his palms. As though he knew what they wanted, he spread his hands out flat and rotated his palms slowly over the taut peaks.

Charlotte gasped, then groaned.

He kept up the rotating motion till her breasts were swollen and her nipples so sensitive that the sensations he created were close to pain.

Just when she felt she could bear it no longer, he stopped. Perversely, she opened her mouth to protest. But before she could utter a word, he spun her in his arms and covered her mouth with his own.

His lips were hard, and hungry, his hands on her back just as demanding. He clamped her to him, kept her lips open and drove his tongue deep. Charlotte had thought he'd kissed her with passion in the lobby. But this…this was more than a kiss. This was total ravishment.

His reefing away both startled and dismayed her. Her eyes flew open to find him taking a backward step from her and running an agitated hand through his hair. His face was flushed and his breathing ragged.

'What's wrong?' she asked.

He stared at her, before shaking his head, then smiling a rather wry smile.

'I was going way too fast.'

'But I liked you going fast.'

'You wouldn't in the end.'

'How do you know?'

'I know.' He smiled another of those wry smiles.

'Sheikhs know these things. Now I suggest you go get the rest of that dress off by yourself. Take a shower. And put on something more comfortable. Both our bags should be in the dressing room leading off from the bathroom. Or so I was told.'

Charlotte didn't want to do any of those things. She wanted to stay with him and have him kiss her some more. And play with her some more, then just take her, without too much preamble. Her nipples were still hard but the rest of her body was in melt-down mode. She wanted him.

But she would not beg.

'I won't be long,' she said, hurrying into the bath-room and shutting the door behind her.

The sight of herself in the huge vanity mirror was a shock. How decadent she looked standing there, half-naked. Spinning away, she hurried into the ad-joining dressing room, where she stripped off the rest of her clothes, not returning to the bathroom till she was totally naked.

As she walked over to the vanity to get one of the complimentary shower caps, she glanced at herself in the mirror again.

Louise always said she had a fabulous body. Charlotte thought it was good, but not fabulous. Her hips were a bit wide. But she looked in proportion and she'd never felt ashamed of it.

But she'd been brought up in a modest household where you didn't flaunt yourself. Being totally naked in front of *anyone* had always been a problem with her, but especially the opposite sex. Mostly, in the past, she would undress then dive into bed and keep under the sheets.

Charlotte had long ago realised her inhibitions were a contributing factor in the ultimate failure of all her relationships, especially the one with Dwayne.

Strangely, though, she did not feel any of her usual shyness with Daniel. She wanted him to see her naked. Wanted him to make love to her, to be inventive.

Her hands lifted to lightly touch her nipples, producing a delicious quiver. She did it again, then cupped her whole breasts as Daniel had.

Her responses rocked Charlotte. Daniel wasn't even here and she was finding pleasure in her body.

Louise was right. This had to be lust, not love.

It was a liberating realisation, because she didn't want to love Daniel. She did, however, want to make love with him.

The bathroom door suddenly opening behind her had her snatching her hands away from her still throbbing breasts and whirling round.

'I didn't hear the shower,' Daniel said as he entered and walked towards her, seemingly unaware of being totally naked. Not so Charlotte. Her mouth went dry at the sight of him.

'Why don't we share?' he asked, and with one smoothly sweeping action scooped her up into his arms.

Charlotte didn't object. How could she? She was having enough trouble just breathing.

He held her with one hand whilst he turned on both taps in the made-for-two shower, adjusting the temperature and the shower heads till he was satisfied. Then he lowered her carefully to that spot where the two sprays met in the middle.

'My hair,' she did protest when the warm water started streaming down over her head.

'Don't worry about your hair,' he commanded, and pulled her against him again, not quite so roughly as the last time. But there was still an intensity in his body language which Charlotte found incredibly exciting. She liked to think he wasn't quite as cool as usual, that she had rattled him today.

She could feel his hardness pressed against her stomach, evoking wild images in her imagination.

'Are we going to do it here?' she asked him breathlessly.

He frowned down at her. 'Do you want to?'

'Yes.'

'Hell, Charlotte.'

'What?'

'You have to stop doing this to me.'

'Doing what?'

'Making me lose the plot. I'm the sheikh here. You're the captive bride. You do as *I* say.'

'Do I have to? I mean…I don't want to wait.'

'You might not have noticed but I'm not wearing a condom. They're back in the bedroom. Can't you wait a few minutes?'

She really couldn't.

'Unless there's some other reason why you have to use protection,' she blurted out, 'I—er—I'm on the Pill.'

'On the Pill,' he repeated, and a shudder ran

through him. 'You shouldn't have told me that, Charlotte.'

'Why not?'

'Because men will often say anything not to use condoms. Men can be very selfish. And stupid. I've always used protection myself. I'm somewhat paranoid about getting a girl pregnant. But you only have my word for that.'

'Your word is fine by me,' she said. 'I know you wouldn't lie about something as serious as that.'

'God, woman.'

'What?'

'Nothing.' He shook his head, splashing water all over the place. 'This is going to be a new experience for me.'

'What is?'

'Being with someone like you.'

'What does that mean? What's different about me?'

'Everything. Now shut up and let me kiss you.'

She shut up and let him kiss her and kiss her till she was squirming against him. Once again, his mouth burst away, his eyes flashing her a warning.

'Enough of that,' he growled, and spun her in his arms so that her back was to him. The water splashed down over her head and body, forming rivulets that streamed down.

'Wind your arms back around my waist,' he told her.

It was an incredibly exciting position, leaving her entire front totally accessible to his hands whilst hers were linked behind him as if she was, indeed, a captive bride. She could feel her heart thudding behind her ribs, her chest rising and falling.

Her heart raced even more when he dribbled shower gel over her breasts then started to caress them. The slipperiness of the liquid soap made everything more sensual and sensitive. Soft little sounds of pleasure escaped her lips every time he grazed one of her nipples.

When he abandoned her breasts and moved southward, Charlotte sucked in her stomach. When he passed beyond her navel, her whole belly started quivering. He was going to touch her down there. Her breath caught in anticipation and then his hand was sliding into the slickened folds of her sex. Every internal muscle she owned tensed, and waited. Waited and craved. His fingers slowly slid inside, moving as deep as they could before withdrawing a little then pushing deep again.

And again. And again.

Her breath began coming in short, sharp pants. Something was happening inside her. He kept touching something with each inward push, then sweeping over another highly sensitive part as he withdrew. Blinding pleasure mingled with an escalating frustration, a need for something that remained just outside her reach. Her muscles tightened further. Her mouth fell open. She wanted to scream. Or sob.

'Oh,' she cried out when the first spasm hit. 'Oh…'

Charlotte had always tried to imagine what an orgasm felt like. Nothing in her mind, however, matched the reality of the experience.

But how *could* you describe such feelings? Or the sensations? They were beyond words.

'Good?' he whispered in her ear when it was over.

'Mmm,' was all she could reply. Suddenly she went all limp, her arms flopping back down to her sides.

'Too tired to continue?'

'Not at all,' she shot back, snapping out of her momentary exhaustion in a hurry. No way was she going to waste any of tonight. Not if she could help it.

'In that case, I think we should adjourn to the bed.'

She swung round to face him. 'But I don't want to go to bed.' As much as the bed out there looked incredibly romantic and erotic, bed had never been a place where sex for her had been all that successful. She liked being in this shower with him. It excited her. 'I'd much prefer to stay here for a while.'

'Actual sex in the shower is not always a good idea, Charlotte,' he said. 'Not unless…' His black eyes glittered momentarily. But then he shook his head. 'No. No, I don't think so.'

'But I want to,' she insisted, her hands lifting to rest on his chest. 'Tell me what to do. *Show* me.'

Show her.

Daniel groaned. Didn't she know he was already close to the point of no return?

His male ego had been pleased with having made her come. But it demanded more. He wanted her to climax whilst he was making love to her. But that was unlikely if he proceeded at this stage. He'd come himself in no time and she'd be left in no man's land.

But he was tempted. Cruelly tempted.

'It's too soon,' he told her. 'For *you*.'

'But not for you,' she returned, her eyes dropping to where he was still erect.

'No,' he said ruefully. 'Not for me.'

He almost jumped out of his skin when she reached down and curled both her hands around him.

'No, don't,' he warned her. But she was already caressing him, moving her soft hands up and down his aching shaft. When she moved a thumbpad over the velvety tip, he groaned.

'Good?' she whispered, an echo of what he'd asked her earlier.

'Yes,' he bit out.

He grimaced when she reached for the shower gel and poured some over him. Hell on earth!

Now her hands slid so easily up and down. Up and down. Up and down.

'Charlotte,' he choked out.

She looked up into his eyes. Hers were big and gleaming with a wild excitement. She was genuinely enjoying what she was doing, this realisation shattering what little was left of his control.

He still tried to stop himself. This was not what he intended. He'd been going to be the master here, and she the pupil. It was clear, however, that she was not as inexperienced as Brad had intimated, for she sure as hell had done this before.

'Yes,' she ground out with elation in her eyes when he started to tremble. 'Yes…'

CHAPTER THIRTEEN

'How do you take your coffee?' Charlotte asked, glancing over at Daniel.

He was sprawled out on one of the sofas, eating grapes, his upper torso bare, a bath sheet slung low around his hips.

Charlotte was wearing one of the hotel's white towelling bathrobes. She'd spotted her overnight bag in the dressing room when she'd stripped off earlier, but hadn't bothered to open it yet.

'Black. One sugar,' he replied.

'I wish I had a rubber band,' she muttered as she made them both coffee. 'I'd like to get this hair out of my face.' Still damp, her hair was a heavy mass of wayward waves that fell across one eye all the time. She pushed it back and tried to anchor it behind her ear, not altogether successfully.

'Don't be silly. Your hair looks great like that. Very sexy. Like you.'

Charlotte flushed. 'You honestly think I'm sexy?'

'Do you doubt me?'

'I'm different from usual with you,' she confessed as she carried over the two mugs and placed them down on the black-lacquered coffee-table. 'I don't make a habit of doing what I did in the shower. In fact, I've never done anything like that before.'

But she'd wanted to. That was the most shocking

thing of all. She didn't just feel sexier with him, she felt wicked. Lust had turned her from her usual reserved self into a vamp.

'You are constantly surprising me, Charlotte,' he said as he picked up his coffee mug, his eyes meeting hers over the rim.

Lord, but he had incredible eyes. His body wasn't too bad, either.

Not too hard. Not too soft. Just right.

Like baby bear's bed.

Charlotte smiled at this unlikely simile. There was nothing babyish about Daniel.

'What's so amusing?' he asked.

'Nothing.'

'Don't go all mysterious on me. I like it that you're so honest and open.'

'I was thinking what a great body you have,' she confessed.

He actually looked surprised by her compliment.

'It's adequate enough. The person in this room with the really great body is you.'

She flushed. 'Flatterer.'

'Don't be coy. You must know you look great in the buff.'

'My bottom's too big,' she protested.

He laughed. 'I don't think too many men would agree. I certainly don't. You have a delicious bottom. And beautiful breasts. And fabulous legs. Or so I recall,' he added, a devilish smile playing around his mouth. 'Why don't you take off that robe so that I can see it all again, make sure I wasn't mistaken?'

She froze, the mug at her lips. 'Out here?' she choked out, her heart stopping in its tracks.

OK, so the lighting was soft and romantic, but the curtains were wide open, and whilst it didn't look as if anyone could see in, how could she be sure? There were lots of high-rise buildings down this end of town, and lots had lights on in the windows.

'Why not out here?'

'M...maybe when I finish this coffee,' she stammered.

'Now would be better. Then I could look at you whilst we drink.'

Her hands shook as she lowered the mug to the coffee-table. Did she dare? Had she become *that* wicked?

It seemed she had.

Her thighs trembled as she stood up, but a second glance over at the tinted window reassured her that no one could see anything at that distance.

The looped sash of her robe undid with the slightest of pulls, the sides falling apart. His eyes narrowed but he didn't stop sipping his coffee. In fact, he leant right back against the sofa in an attitude of total relaxation.

Charlotte was far from relaxed. This was what it must feel like, she imagined, just before diving off one of those high boards.

She sucked in a deep breath, then shrugged the robe off her shoulders. It fell to the floor, leaving her feeling more naked than she ever had in her life.

Not just her body but her very soul. Both were

naked before him, this man who could make her do things and feel things that no man had before.

He put his mug down and just drank her in. Slowly.

'Beautiful,' was all he said, but it left her shaken.

Because she knew in that telling moment that she would do anything he asked her to do.

'Why don't you sit down and finish your coffee?'

His suggestion—delivered oh, so coolly—confirmed what Charlotte already suspected, which was that Daniel was far more sophisticated than any man she'd ever been with. Clearly, he was used to playing erotic games like this, in having women do his bidding in the bedroom.

Maybe that was what was turning her on so much. Not just his handsome face and great body but also his suave know-how; that air of supreme confidence that clung to him in everything he did.

Hadn't Louise said this was what she needed, to have an older man teach her everything?

Daniel wasn't all that much older than her in age but he sure was in experience.

Silly of her to waste a moment of the time she spent with him.

'I don't think I'll be wanting any more coffee,' she said, her voice sounding determined.

He raised one eyebrow before putting down his own coffee, then stripping the towel from around his hips. 'Best come over here, then, don't you think?' he said, tossing the towel aside and lightly slapping one of his muscular thighs.

Her knees felt like jelly but she went, mouth dry

and heart racing, her belly tightening as she settled her shapely bottom across his lap and wound her arms around his neck.

'No, this way,' he instructed, and lifted her round till she was straddling his thighs, their faces almost level. His eyes held hers as he took hold of her hips and eased her up onto her knees.

Charlotte sucked in air sharply.

His hands slid round behind her knees, gently drawing them forwards, causing her to slowly sink downwards and take him in, inch by glorious inch.

She could have wept with pleasure. He was buried very deep inside her, filling her entirely. She loved the feeling, but was anxious for more.

'What now?' she asked tautly.

His brows drew together. 'Are you saying you haven't done this before either?'

'Not on a sofa. And never very well.'

'Use your knees to lift your bottom up and down, like you're riding a horse. Have you ever ridden a horse?'

'Please. I'm country.'

Charlotte could not believe she could sound so calm and casual at such a moment. No doubt she was keen to impress him, if not with her sexual expertise, then her willingness to learn.

Her hands curled over his shoulders, her nails digging in as she started to rise and fall.

What had felt wonderful inside her in repose, now felt incredible. She could not get enough of the sensation of being filled by him, over and over. Those frantic feelings returned, stronger this time and more compelling. She began to move faster.

His raw moan brought her to a fearful halt. She'd hurt him. Oh, she was hopeless.

'No, don't stop.' His voice was hoarse, his face anguished. 'Just keep doing what you're doing. It feels fantastic. *You're* fantastic.'

She happily obeyed, closing her eyes in an effort to concentrate. But it became increasingly difficult to focus on anything but the tension building inside her. Her belly tightened. Her thighs quivered. Her heart stopped. Then suddenly she was there, splintering apart around him, practically sobbing with the intensity of her release.

He cried out at the same time and for the first time Charlotte understood what it meant to be as one. They were fused together, flesh within flesh, both shuddering in ecstasy at the same time. She was still contracting around him when his hands cupped her face and drew her gasping mouth down to his, kissing her till their mutual pleasure died away.

Only then did his lips leave hers.

'*More* than fantastic,' he murmured, his eyes heavily hooded with spent passion.

When he gathered her close to his heart, she sighed a deeply contented sigh, her mind and body already beginning to shut down.

'Enough for now,' he said as he smoothed his hand up and down her spine. 'Go to sleep, sweet Charlotte.'

'I don't want to sleep,' she mumbled.

'Don't worry. I'll wake you up later.'

'Promise?'

'Cross my heart and hope to die.'

'Don't take me to bed,' she told him, sounding for all the world as if she was drugged.

'Why not?' He sounded startled.

'Not the bed. Not yet. Promise.'

'Crazy girl. All right. I promise.'

'Good.'

CHAPTER FOURTEEN

CHARLOTTE woke slowly, drifting out of a deep haze of sleep that seemed to want to drag her back and cocoon her forever. She yawned. Stretched. Then, finally, opened her eyes.

The first thing she saw was herself in the ceiling mirror. And Daniel next to her. Still fast asleep.

He was sprawled face down, the white satin sheet covering him up to the waist, his arms folded under the pillow on which his head rested.

Charlotte caught herself smiling. She should have felt wrecked. Instead, she felt wonderful.

A glance at her wrist-watch showed that it was twenty past ten. Not all that late considering she'd been awake most of the night.

And what a night!

If she hadn't been at this moment looking at Daniel's real-life reflection, she might have thought it was all a dream. Rolling over, Charlotte placed a kiss of gratitude on his nearest shoulder, rubbing her lips lightly back and forth across his skin.

He didn't stir. Understandable. The man had to be exhausted.

He'd been incredible last night. The kind of lover women fantasised about but rarely ever experienced. He knew exactly what to do to turn her on, and to keep her there. He'd made love to her in ways she hadn't even read about.

He made a better sheikh than she could've ever imagined. Dominating and demanding at times, but wonderfully tender at others. He seemed to know exactly what she needed to obliterate her sexual history. With him, there'd been no sign of the rather timid, fearful lover she'd become over the years. Any tension she felt with Daniel had been strictly sexual. She did so love the way he had mercilessly taken her to the edge, wickedly leaving her there till she begged him for deliverance from her torment.

But it was a delicious torment. She loved it, really.

Charlotte would have liked to stay there in the bed, reliving every delicious moment in her mind, but nature was calling, and so was their lack of time. Of course, Daniel had suggested again at one particularly satisfying moment that he come with her up to the Hunter Valley today. And of course this time she'd said, yes, please.

If she was still worried at the back of her mind that her newly discovered desire might deepen to something else, her worry was not as strong as her need. Having Daniel make love to her some more was worth the risk of some heartbreak afterwards. Worth just about any risk, to be honest. Such was the power of her passion for him, and the pleasure he could deliver.

Charlotte wasn't sure what time checkout was, but even if it was late checkout at twelve, that didn't give them all that much time. Besides, she wanted to make herself perfect for Daniel before he woke.

Careful not to disturb him, she climbed out of the bed and tiptoed to the bathroom.

Daniel woke to the sound of the shower running. With a groan, he rolled over and checked the time on his watch, which was lying on the black-lacquered bedside table. Ten-thirty.

Checkout wasn't till twelve. Time enough for a decent breakfast. He was sure Room Service would organise something. This was the bridal suite, after all.

And it was worth every penny, he thought with a satisfied smile as he lifted the phone next to the bed. Charlotte had finally agreed to his coming with her up to the Hunter Valley today, giving him a few more days to convince her that he wanted her for more than a holiday fling. He wondered if she would consider coming back to America and living with him...

'Housekeeping,' a woman's voice answered when he punched in the number six.

'This is Mr Bannister in the Arabian Nights suite. We'd like to order some breakfast.'

'Yes, of course, Mr Bannister. What would you like? Lots of newlyweds opt for the champagne breakfast.'

'I don't think so.' They'd had more than enough champagne last night. 'We need something far more substantial this morning. We'll have muesli, freshly squeezed orange juice, bacon and eggs, wholemeal toast and brewed coffee.'

'Yes, Mr Bannister. And when would you like that delivered?'

'Make it eleven.' That gave him time to shower and shave.

'Very good, sir.'

Daniel hung up, got up and glanced around for something to put on, but there was nothing but the clothes he'd worn the day before. His bag was in the dressing room and the only access to that was through the bathroom. Not wanting to burst in on Charlotte again, he strode out to the sitting area, where he knew he'd left a towel during the night.

As he swept it up from where it was spread over the coffee-table, images flashed back into his mind of an abandoned Charlotte spread out across that table whilst he'd made love to her.

Daniel's chest contracted at the memory of how it had felt, taking her like that. It had been wild. *She'd* been wild.

For a girl with so little experience, Charlotte had been very quick to embrace the delights of the flesh. If Daniel had any worries this morning, they lay in the fact that sex might be the only thing Charlotte would ever want from him. However, she'd been quite adamant the other day about wanting marriage and children, and having no intention of settling for less.

Which rather left Daniel in a dilemma. Because no way was he marrying any woman, no matter how much he loved her!

Daniel froze, with the towel dangling in front of him.

Love. He *loved* her.

Well, of course you do, you idiot, came the ex-asperated voice of long-ignored logic. Why else do you think you've been acting the way you have? Pursuing her like some madman. Going through with that pretend wedding. Turning yourself inside out last night to make her feel fulfilled.

No man does all that if he's not in love!

Daniel slumped down on the nearest sofa, stunned. Somehow, admitting that he loved her changed everything. And forced him to face a fear far greater than his fear of marriage.

What if Charlotte never loved him back? What if, after the next few days were over, she said 'Goodbye, Daniel. Thanks for all the great sex. Off you go, lover. No, sorry, I don't want your love and I don't want you. I want a man capable of true caring and commitment, not some man who has no confidence in himself being a good husband and father'?

Daniel bristled at these imagined insults. Of *course* he could make a good husband and father. Now that he realised he was capable of love, he was capable of anything!

His sigh carried relief. That felt better. Much better. In fact, once the idea of marrying Charlotte took hold, Daniel liked it a lot. He even liked the idea of having children with her. She'd make a wonderful mother.

One problem still remained, however. Getting Charlotte to fall in love with him. Lusting after him was one thing, love something entirely different. He knew that now.

Daniel might have succumbed to a crisis of confidence if his male ego hadn't galloped to the rescue.

You've had no trouble getting women to fall in love with you in the past, he was reminded. You have a hell of a lot going for you.

Still, it might help to tell Charlotte he'd fallen in love with her, and that he'd changed his mind about getting married.

He would have to pick his moment, however. Not too soon. She might not believe him. No, he would have to wait. Meanwhile…

Daniel stood up, wrapped the towel around his hips and headed for the bathroom. The sound of water running had stopped. Hopefully Charlotte was dressed by now. Still, he would knock and make sure.

Charlotte was about to start blow-drying her hair when a firm tap came on the bathroom door.

'Yes?'

'I've ordered breakfast for eleven,' Daniel called through the door. 'I need to shower and shave before then. Are you finished in there?'

She wasn't. Not even remotely. But the hair-dryer wasn't one of those connected to the wall, so she could finish her face and hair elsewhere. There was a carved wooden desk in the sitting area, she'd noted last night, with a gilt-edged mirror on the wall above it. That could serve as a dressing table.

But she was disappointed that Daniel would see her as Louise did most mornings. She'd wanted to be all made up for him, with her hair looking as if she'd just stepped out of a salon.

Oh, well. At least she had a new outfit on, one of the ones she'd bought to wear on her honeymoon. Crisp white hipster jeans—the stretch kind that clung and didn't crush—teamed with a buttercup-yellow halter-necked top and white slip-on sandals. Strappy ones with sexy little heels.

Thinking of sex brought Charlotte's mind to her underwear, which was very sexy but not altogether comfortable. Her bra was a silky cream push-up number she'd bought in that expensive lingerie shop. There was a matching G-string with a lace edging, which looked great.

Picking up the hair-dryer and her toilet bag, Charlotte reluctantly clip-clopped across the black marble floor and opened the door.

Daniel tried not to stare at her. Love, they often said, was blind. In his case, however, it was anything but. As he looked down into her freshly washed face and clear blue eyes, he was overcome with emotion.

He almost told her he loved her right then and there.

Instead he swore, which brought a startled glance to her beautiful eyes.

'Sorry,' he apologised rather grumpily. 'But you have no right to look so damned gorgeous this morning. You should be all bleary-eyed. Like me.'

Bleary-eyed! Was he kidding? He looked scrumptious, that designer stubble on his chin only adding to his sex appeal. As did his only having a towel draped around his hips. Daniel had a great upper body, with broad shoulders, well-defined pecs and a flat, hard stomach.

Charlotte knew she was staring at the man quite shamelessly. But she didn't care. She was totally besotted.

'I've been thinking,' she said. Anything to get her mind off ripping that towel off him, right here and now. 'What's your sister going to say to your going away with me today? I mean…she's the one you've come all this way to visit, after all.'

'She won't mind,' he returned abruptly. 'I can always extend my visit.'

Charlotte's heart jumped at this news. 'Really? I thought you had to return to LA in a fortnight.'

He shrugged. 'I'm my own boss.'

'Oh. I see. Good. I wouldn't want you getting into trouble because of me.' And with a supreme effort of will she pushed past him. 'All yours,' she said blithely over her shoulder as she walked off.

Once the bathroom door was safely shut behind her and she heard the shower taps snap on, Charlotte bolted for the other room, dropping her things on one of the sofas and picking up the phone. Once she had an outside line she punched in her home number. She simply had to talk to Louise, had to have some common sense talked to her. And fast!

'Yes,' a foggy voice answered.

'Louise, it's me. Wake up.'

'Charlotte! Brad, it's Charlotte!'

'I don't want a three-way conversation, thanks,'

Charlotte said sharply. 'I want to talk to you and only you.'

She heard some muffled sounds in the background before Louise came back on the line.

'I'm on my way to the kitchen right now. Shoot!'

'Tell me again it's only lust.'

'Oooh. That good, eh?'

'Yes.'

'Then it's definitely only lust. A specially addictive kind. There'll be no going back now, sweetie.'

'So you don't think I've fallen in love with the man?'

'Nah. What's to love?'

Charlotte could think of many things to love about Daniel. He wasn't just a stud. He was kind, and intelligent, and sensitive, and successful, and generous.

Her heart contracted as she thought of how he'd given her father all that money. Thousands, it must have been. He needn't have done that. She'd been angry at the time but that had been *her* problem, not Daniel's. She must have seemed awfully ungrateful to him.

'Hey there!' Louise said. 'Why so quiet all of a sudden?'

'No reason. Louise, could you do me a favour?'

'Anything.'

'Pack a bag for me. There's a navy sports bag in the bottom of my wardrobe. Throw in all those new clothes I bought for my honeymoon. And whatever accessories you think I'll need. I already have my make-up, perfume and toiletries with me, so you don't have to worry about those. I'll be by to pick it up around twelve-thirty.'

'I won't be here by then. Brad's taking me to his house for a barbeque.'

'Oh…'

'Don't worry, I'll pack it and leave it near the front door. Gosh, I'm so glad last night was a success, but I can't stay and chat. Not if I have to pack you a bag and get ready myself. Brad's just come in and given me strict orders to hurry.'

'That's fine. Thanks, Louise.'

'No sweat. Take care.'

Louise hung up with Brad still looking impatiently at her. He came forward and pulled her into his arms. 'Forget the coffee and come back to bed.'

'I can't. I have to pack Charlotte a bag before we go.'

'Why can't she pack her own bag?'

'Because she wants to get lover-boy up to the Hunter Valley as soon as possible, I guess. Have some more of whatever she had last night.'

'And you don't?' He looked offended.

'I would have thought after six months of continual sex you'd have had enough by now.'

'I'll never have enough of you, babe. When are you going to realise that?'

Louise didn't reply. Impossible with Brad's mouth clamped solidly over hers. But underneath his kiss, her heart was doing strange things. Damn that wedding yesterday. It made a girl want things. And think things. And feel things.

Maybe the time had come to give love another chance.

CHAPTER FIFTEEN

'I'M SORRY about this, sis,' Daniel said as he hastily repacked the clothes he'd unpacked a couple of days earlier. 'I know you must be disappointed.'

'Yes, and no,' Beth replied.

Daniel flicked her a questioning glance. 'Meaning?'

'I *had* been looking forward to your stay. I won't deny it. I've been lonely since I gave up work to have this baby. But I'm willing to sacrifice the immediate pleasure of your company for the long term.'

Daniel zipped up his natty travelling case then glanced up at his sister again. 'Meaning?'

She smiled. 'I know my big brother well enough to know when he's finally fallen in love.'

Daniel's smile was wry. 'Have I been *that* obvious?'

'Afraid so. Vince said it was written all over your face at the wedding. Says he's never seen a groom so much in love with a bride.'

'It took *me* a while to realise the truth. But when I did, I have to tell you, Beth, I was blown away. True love's pretty powerful, isn't it?'

Her eyes went all soft. 'Yes, Daniel. It is.'

'I'd do anything for her.'

'I can see that.'

He sighed. 'I'm worried Charlotte might never feel

the same way. I mean…this could all be rebound stuff.' He didn't like to say he thought it might be just sex.

'Could be,' Beth replied. 'She must have at least *thought* she was in love with that other man, if she was going to marry him. But she's obviously very attracted to you. The girl I met on Friday would not be taking you with her on her honeymoon if her own feelings weren't pretty powerful. She didn't strike me as the promiscuous type.'

'She's not,' Daniel agreed, feeling marginally better with Beth's reminder of Charlotte's good character.

'Then be careful, Daniel. She has to be confused right now. She's going to need time to sort out her feelings.'

'How much time?'

'You'll have to play it by ear, darling. Just be your usual confident, charming self and I'm sure she'll be yours in the end.'

Daniel wasn't so sure. Charlotte was different from every woman he'd ever been with. She didn't seem all that impressed with his charm. Or his wealth. She only seemed interested in his body.

Which was certainly putting the boot on the other foot. In the past, that was all he'd been interested in when it came to women. Sex. Most of them hadn't liked being reduced to sex objects. He could now understand exactly how they felt.

'Charlotte inferred over breakfast that after this honeymoon holiday was over, we were over.'

'Maybe she's protecting herself. She thinks you're

the love 'em and leave 'em type, so she's getting in first.'

Daniel glared at Beth. 'She wouldn't have thought that if you hadn't said as much.'

'Come, now, Daniel, you have playboy written all over you. Any man who looks like you, has money and is still a bachelor at thirty-six is automatically tagged by women as a good-time guy. Your Charlotte is no dummy. She's been around. She would make her own assessment of you.'

Daniel grimaced. 'Yeah, you're right. I even told her myself I was allergic to marriage.'

'You certainly dug your own grave with that one. The girl wants marriage above all, and children. Most of us do, eventually. You have to let her know you've changed your mind about commitment and marriage. Give her a chance to fall in love with you.'

Daniel pulled a face. 'I want her to fall in love with me for myself. Not because I'm dangling the carrot of marriage.'

Beth sighed. 'You always did want it all, Daniel.'

'No, Beth, I just don't want what Dad has these days. I want the real thing. Charlotte is the real thing.'

'Then go get it.'

Charlotte sat in the car outside Beth's house, waiting impatiently for him to reappear. She'd refused to accompany him inside whilst he packed some things for their trip. She would have felt awkward in front of his sister and her husband.

What must they be thinking of her?

It was one thing to go through with a pretend wedding, quite another to take the pretend groom away with her on her honeymoon.

Charlotte had never condoned casual sex. Or fast women. Yet here she was, being faster than fast. And loving it.

After talking to Louise this morning, she'd momentarily wondered again if she had fallen in love with Daniel. But when he emerged from the bathroom, looking sinfully sexy in cool beige trousers and a wine-coloured silk shirt, Charlotte had accepted the reality that desire was the main catalyst propelling her uncharacteristic behaviour.

She could not wait to go with Daniel to the resort. To have him all to herself. For five whole days!

Despite not wanting to face his sister right now, Charlotte steadfastly refused to let guilt, or shame, or worry spoil her excitement. She would keep all those negative emotions till the honeymoon was over. Meanwhile, she was going to enjoy every incredible moment.

Her heart leapt when the gate in the high security wall surrounding Beth's house swung open and Daniel walked through, pulling a compact black travelling case behind him.

Flicking the lock on her hatchback, she leapt out from behind the wheel and hurried round to open it for him.

He smiled one of his heart-stopping smiles as he joined her. 'I must have the most beautiful chauffeur in Sydney,' he complimented, swinging his case in beside hers before bending to kiss her on the mouth.

Just a light kiss but it sent her heart racing.

Their eyes met, with his seeming to search hers.

'What?' she said.

'Nothing. Shall we go?'

'What did your sister say?' she asked once they were on their way. 'Was she angry?'

'No. A little disappointed. But I promised to make it up to her.'

'How?'

'Like I said before, I'll stay on a while longer.'

Charlotte wasn't sure she liked the sound of that. What if he wanted to keep seeing her? She knew she could not help falling for him if things went on, and on, and on.

Just keep concentrating on the sexual side of things, she advised herself, a task that was all too easy at the moment. Just having Daniel sitting beside her in this car focused her mind on the physical. She could smell his tangy aftershave, feel the heat emanating from his body. She kept glancing over at his beautiful hands with their long, strong fingers and thinking of the places she wanted them to stroke and explore and...

'Better watch the road,' he warned sharply when the car drifted towards the next lane. 'Or let me drive.'

'Absolutely not,' she returned, quickly pulling herself—and the car—into line. 'You don't know the way.'

'I'm not a total stranger to Sydney, you know.'

'Maybe, but it's been a while. And you told me

over breakfast you'd never been up north to the Hunter Valley.'

On top of that, she didn't want him tired when they arrived.

'Why don't you lie back and have a rest?' she suggested. 'Not much to see till we get out of the city. Not much then, either, to be honest. The freeway is not renowned for its scenery. It's pretty when we cross the Hawkesbury River but that's about it.'

'Why can't we just talk?' he counter-suggested.

Talk? She didn't want to talk to him. She didn't want to get to know any more about him. She already liked what she knew too much.

'What about?' she asked warily.

He shrugged. 'Anything and everything.'

Her chest tightened. 'I find it hard to concentrate on the traffic and talk.'

'It's Sunday. There's not that much traffic.'

'Yes, well, I'm a nervous driver.'

'Your dad said you weren't the nervous type.'

'Well, I am around you, OK?' she snapped, then wished she hadn't. Keep it cool, Charlotte. 'Look, I'll put the radio on and you can listen to that.'

She turned the car radio on to the BBC, which had a lot of news and chat shows as opposed to music.

'Will that do?'

'It'll have to, I guess.' And he settled back with arms crossed, his eyes half-shut.

Charlotte almost sighed with relief. Though any real relief was short-lived, her mind swiftly back on what was to come later in the day. The clock on the dash said one-fifteen. Check-in time at the resort was three. With a bit of luck they should arrive shortly after three.

And shortly after that?

Charlotte quivered inside at the prospect of being behind closed doors with Daniel once more. She'd been excited yesterday, but nothing like this. Knowing the pleasure in store for her was turning her crazy. She could think of nothing else.

Her hands tightened around the wheel to stop them trembling.

The next two hours, Charlotte suspected, were going to be the longest two hours in her life!

CHAPTER SIXTEEN

DANIEL didn't listen to the radio. His mind was firmly on analysing Charlotte's actions and reactions to him just now.

She was nervous. That much was clear.

What was it her dad had said? Caring makes a person nervous. Did Charlotte's nervousness mean she cared? Or was she just turned on?

Maybe he shouldn't have kissed her back behind the car. But every time he saw her, he was overcome with the need to do something physical.

Damn it all, now *he* felt nervous, which wasn't his usual state of mind. But there was just so much at stake here. Winning Charlotte's heart was going to be a much more difficult mission. Yet giving her good sex was all he could do for a while.

Not that this prospect was unpleasant. Hell, he couldn't even *think* about making love to Charlotte without getting aroused. She was just so responsive. And so obviously delighted that she'd finally found the joy of sex. It was only natural that she'd want to experience everything.

A surreptitious sidewards glance showed she was quite pink in the cheeks. Possibly nervous *and* excited.

And so damned beautiful.

He really loved the way she'd done her hair today,

yet it was totally different from yesterday at the wedding. This time it was scraped back very tightly from her face and secured in a high ponytail. The ponytail wasn't at all girlish, or wavy. It was sleek and chic and very sexy, the style exposing her elegant neck and drawing his eye to her dangling earrings.

They were silver, and diamond-shaped, with small pearls hanging off each point. Every time the car went round a corner, they swung from side to side.

Daniel had read a book once on the various erotic zones on a woman's body. The earlobes were one of them. Women since the days of the Pharoahs had drawn attention to their earlobes with earrings to attract the male. And turn him on.

The tactic worked.

'Will you stop staring at me?' she said sharply.

Daniel noted the frustration in her voice, plus her knuckles showing white on the wheel. Plus something else.

'You've taken off Gary's ring,' he pointed out.

'What?'

'Your engagement ring. You've taken it off.' Left the wedding ring on, though, he noted. His was still firmly jammed on *his* finger.

'Oh, yes. The ring. I put it in a drawer when I picked up my things.'

'Are you going to send it back to Gary?' Keep her talking, Daniel.

She sighed. 'I probably will. I know what he did was weak and wrong, but I'm not proving much better, am I?'

'I wouldn't say that.'

She laughed. 'No, you wouldn't. You probably do things like this all the time. But I don't. Still, I'm not going to beat myself up over it. I'm here with you because I want to be. Nobody's twisting my arm.'

'You make it sound like what we're doing is sordid. You're free as a bird, Charlotte. You have a right to be with whoever you want to be.'

'You don't think people might think I'm shallow and promiscuous to go from wanting to marry Gary one day to sleeping with you the next?'

Daniel frowned. Beth was right. Charlotte was feeling very mixed-up. And not totally comfortable with her decision to come away with him.

'That's over-simplifying what is really a more complex situation than that,' he said carefully. 'You didn't love Gary, for starters.'

'No. But I thought I did. I'm always thinking I'm in love with men when I'm not.'

Daniel's heart missed a beat. Was that a slip of the tongue? Did she mean him? He sure hoped not. But this was not the right time to press. All he could do was soothe her conscience, and her fears over looking shallow or promiscuous.

'Lots of people think they're in love when they're not,' he began. Hell no, he shouldn't have said that.

Her laugh was dry. 'I've finally realised that. If I'd met you at any other time in my life, I might have thought I'd fallen for you. At least I've grown up enough now to know it's just a sex thing, like it is for you with me.'

Oh, terrific! Now what could he say? But it's not

just a sex thing with me, Charlotte. I love you. I've loved you from the first moment I saw you.

She'd laugh, or accuse him of lying.

'A lot of successful relationships start with sexual attraction,' he remarked instead.

'Obviously not with you. I'll bet you've never even lived with a girl.'

'You're right. I haven't. But maybe that's because I hadn't met the right girl before.'

She shot him a dry look. 'Oh, please, not that old chestnut. You said you liked it that *I* was open and honest. Well, I like it when you are. You're a good-time guy, Daniel. You admitted as much. Which is fine by me, because I want a good time for the next few days. With you.'

Daniel decided then and there to stop rushing things. It was clear he was going to have to be very patient in his mission to marry Charlotte. But that was all right. He had time. She wasn't going anywhere.

'Well, if you want a good time later today,' he said nonchalantly, 'I think I might have to lie back and have that rest you suggested. I'm still a bit knackered from last night.'

CHAPTER SEVENTEEN

CHARLOTTE could not believe it when he not only put his seat right back, but he actually seemed to go to sleep, leaving her with nothing to distract her from her X-rated thoughts but the road and the radio.

After what seemed like an eternity, Charlotte turned off the freeway onto the side-road that led to Cessnock and the lower Hunter Valley. The clock on the dash said two forty-five. If Charlotte had been made to guess the time, she would have said it was much later.

She bitterly resented Daniel's sleeping, which was perverse, since that was what she'd suggested. But she hated him being so cool about everything when she felt like a cat on a hot tin roof.

He suddenly stirred in the seat, popping his seat back up straight and glancing around. 'Where in hell are we?' he said. 'We seem to have been on the road for hours.'

His impatience pleased her.

'Not far now,' she said.

'Thank goodness. Boy, it looks dry out there,' he said, staring out at the countryside.

Actually, Charlotte thought it didn't look too bad for the last month in summer. The grass alongside the road was quite green. Admittedly, the paddocks beyond were somewhat brown in parts and the trees had that thirsty look they got at the end of a hot day, their leaves drooping towards the ground.

'If you think this looks dry, you should see my dad's place. Not a blade of grass in some of the paddocks. He's been hand-feeding his stock for months.'

'What's his water situation like? I was reading the paper at Beth's the other morning, and it said some of the smaller towns are having to ship in water.'

'Water's always a problem in the bush in a long drought. Fortunately, Dad does have a bore well, and a couple of dams. But he'll probably use some of the money you gave him to put in another dam. And replace some of the breeding stock he's had to sell.'

'You're not still angry with me about that money, are you?'

'No,' she said. 'To be honest, I feel bad about the way I reacted to that. You didn't have to do what you did. I realised later you must have known I'd go to bed with you without it.'

The expression on his face was priceless. 'Are you saying you thought I gave your father that money as a bribe to get you to sleep with me?'

'It did cross my mind.'

'But I told your dad not to tell anyone! It's not my fault that he did.'

'I appreciate that now, Daniel. I wasn't thinking straight at the time. I was under a lot of stress. I'm sorry.'

'Apology accepted,' he grumbled, though still not looking too happy. 'But *try*, in future, not to jump to hasty conclusions about me, or judge me so harshly. I am not some depraved roué, Charlotte. I don't even like the term *good-time guy*. I'm just a normal red-blooded man who wants to spend time with a woman he thinks is very beautiful and very special.'

'If you say so,' Charlotte said noncommittally, determined not to be swayed too much, or seduced too far, by Daniel's silver tongue. 'Special, am I? That's sweet.'

'*Sweet!* You make me sound about as substantial as candy floss.'

Charlotte laughed. 'You said that. I didn't. Aah, here we are. Cessnock. Not far to go now. Know anything about Cessnock?'

'Not much.'

He sounded as if he didn't want to know anything, either. But being a tourist guide was nicely distracting.

'Mines, wines and people,' she read aloud from the road sign as they entered the outskirts of Cessnock. 'That just about sums Cessnock up. It was a mining town first. The vineyards came afterwards. In the past few years, that side of this area has boomed.'

'It looks prosperous enough,' he said as they drove slowly down the wide main street.

'It is. Real estate here has gone through the roof. But it *is* a hot spot, especially in the summer. Wait till you get out of this car. The heat outside will take your breath away.' The forecast for the Hunter Valley today had been thirty-eight degrees, much hotter than Sydney's milder climate.

'We're not stopping here, though, are we?'

'No,' she replied.

'How far to go now?' he asked.

'Not far.' The resort had emailed her a map to follow. Which she'd memorised. 'About ten minutes out of town,' she told him. 'Provided I don't take a wrong turn.'

She didn't take a wrong turn and soon they'd left Cessnock behind and were travelling along the winding, tree-lined road that led to Peacock Park.

'According to the map they sent me,' she said, 'it should be on the right. And soon.'

The road dipped down into a gully then began a steep rise. Suddenly, there it was, on their right, a grand-looking assortment of colonial-style buildings perched on the crest of the hill.

'Impressive,' Daniel said as she drove through the large black wrought-iron gates.

'It was actually built over twenty years ago, according to their website, but it's recently been refurbished and is now considered one of the top five resorts in the Hunter Valley. There's everything here you could possibly want,' she told him as she angled the car into one of the parking bays outside the building marked 'Reception'. 'A five-star restaurant, a bar, an indoor solar-heated pool. Tennis courts. Walking trails. A gym. The luxury rooms—where we'll be staying—have spa baths and private verandas with views over the valley.'

'And air-conditioning, I hope,' Daniel said as they both climbed out of the car. 'I see what you mean. This is seriously hot.'

'I did warn you. But it looks like a storm is on the way,' she said, glancing over to the horizon, where a mass of white thunderheads loomed over the mountain range.

But it wasn't only in the sky that a storm was gathering. Now that they had finally arrived, Charlotte felt herself being swept into a maelstrom of fierce longing. The heat in the air was nothing to the heat inside her.

'I think we should get out of this sun,' Daniel said, taking her arm and propelling her towards Reception.

The booking was in her name, thank heavens, so there was no trouble with the formalities. Within five minutes they had their passkey, along with directions to their room. When asked if they wanted a reservation in the restaurant for tonight, Daniel had briskly answered that no, they would be having Room Service.

Charlotte didn't argue. Room Service was exactly what she wanted. Amongst other things.

It took them another couple of minutes to move the car to the parking bay allotted to their room, which was housed in a block some distance from Reception.

'There's no one in the room next to you, so you will have total privacy,' the receptionist had informed them. 'And the best view. You're also quite close to the pool and the gym. Just follow the signs along the path.'

Their room was the end one in a rectangular block that had a high-pitched roof and verandas front and back.

'Would you like to go for a swim till the air-conditioning kicks in?' Daniel asked as he dropped their bags on the veranda outside the room and unlocked the door.

'Would you?' she returned, hating the idea.

'No. A shower would do just as well. If that's all right with you.'

She looked at him, unable to hide the need in her eyes any longer.

'I think you know the answer to that,' she said in a quiet voice, which was all the more powerful for its underlying intensity.

'I feel exactly the same.'

Charlotte would have liked to believe that. But she knew in her heart that Daniel felt nothing even close to what she was feeling. This was a first for her in so many ways. He'd obviously been here, done this before.

He pushed the door open and held it there for her whilst she walked in, rather stunned all of a sudden. It was as though her mind had reached overload. She glanced around the room, superficially noting its style—spacious and country described it best.

'They must have good insulation in here,' Daniel said as he closed the door behind her. 'Has to be ten degrees cooler than outside. But some air-conditioning is still called for.'

He busied himself as men did with all things mechanical and functional, checking out the air-conditioning and the TV which was hidden in a huge wall cabinet across the way from the equally huge bed.

'Great bathroom,' he said after a brief visit there. 'Go check it out.'

She did and he was right. It was fabulous, with a corner spa bath, large shower, double vanities. And every toiletry supplied that any visitor could possibly want.

When she emerged, Daniel had pulled back the curtains that covered the sliding glass doors leading out onto the veranda. He was standing there with his back to her, his legs apart, his hands in his pockets.

'Great view,' he said. 'You can see for miles. Pity we can't go out there yet. Maybe later this evening.'

'Daniel,' Charlotte choked out, unable to bear any further delay.

He turned slowly, his body language showing an odd reluctance to face her.

'Yes, Charlotte?'

'Stop tormenting me.'

He smiled. 'I'm not tormenting you, my darling. I'm tormenting myself.'

His calling her his darling brought a soft moan to her lips. He misinterpreted it, of course, thinking it was an expression of frustration when it was actually a cry of despair. One miserable 'my darling' and all the rubbish about this being nothing but lust was stripped away, leaving her heart raw and bleeding.

He covered the distance between them with three long strides and pulled her roughly into his arms.

She welcomed his lack of gentility. If he'd been tender with her, she might have broken down. Instead, he clamped his mouth over hers quite brutally whilst his hands yanked at her clothes. She helped him, happy to dispense with any actions that smacked of love.

They were naked within no time, naked yet still clawing at each other's flesh. He pushed her back across the bed, spread her legs and drove in deep with a groan.

Suddenly he stopped, staring down at her with strange eyes, as though what he'd just done had shocked him. And maybe it had. Last night he'd been demanding, but never rough.

'Don't stop,' she begged.

Swearing, he hooked her legs high around his back and began to thrust into her.

Charlotte gasped, then groaned, her nails digging into his buttocks as he surged into her over and over. Sweat beaded on his forehead and on hers.

'God, Charlotte,' he moaned at one stage.

'Don't stop,' she replied.

He muttered another four-letter word, and kept on going. But not for long, his face grimacing with something akin to self-disgust as he climaxed.

But he needn't have worried. She came with him, her own face twisting with ecstasy. Or was it agony?

No, no, she refused to go down that self-pitying, self-destructive path, *refused* to believe this was love, no matter how much her silly, romantic soul wanted to believe it was. This was what Louise had told her it was, and nothing more.

Don't look for more. Don't hope for more.

For your sanity's sake, *don't*!

CHAPTER EIGHTEEN

CHARLOTTE stirred to the sound of thunder. The room was almost dark, although the bedside clock showed it was only five-twenty. A flash of lightning was swiftly followed by another rumble of thunder. The storm was very close.

Daniel was not beside her in the bed, but she could see him through the open sliding door. He was sitting out on the veranda, dressed in one of the complimentary bathrobes, sipping a glass of white wine.

The second complimentary robe was draped across the foot of the bed, waiting for her. Daniel must have put it there whilst she'd been asleep. He must have picked her clothes up off the floor as well, because they were lying on a nearby chair, neatly folded.

How kind of him. There again, Daniel *was* kind. Being a good-time guy didn't mean he couldn't be kind.

What a shame that he didn't want marriage. He would make a wonderful husband. Her heart twisted at this last thought, reinforcing what she'd suspected earlier on and which she'd been trying to convince herself wasn't so ever since.

She *did* love the man. Ridiculous to keep denying it.

For a moment, she let her eyes linger lovingly on him.

If only they were really married, and on their real honeymoon. If that were true she could go out there, sit on his lap, share his drink, run her fingers through his hair, tell him he was the handsomest, kindest, sexiest man she'd ever met. There would be no need for *any* pretence. No lies. No embarrassment.

Embarrassment consumed her now as she recalled how she'd clawed at him that first time. But she'd been so desperate with desire.

She still was, despite what had happened afterwards.

Her need for him seemed insatiable, perhaps because sex was her only means of expression. She could not be her natural self with him, or tell him how much she loved him. If she did, he would think her a fickle fool, going from one man to the next all the time, always thinking she was in love with them.

The trouble was this time she really was in love. Sometimes, you had to experience the fool's gold version a couple of times to recognise the real thing when it hit you.

And hit her it had. Like a bulldozer.

Charlotte might have sunk back down under the sheet and pretended to sleep a while longer if nature wasn't calling. With a sigh she rose, slipped into the white towelling robe and padded off to the bathroom, where her eyes inevitably went to the shower cubicle.

The glass walls were still wet from their shower together, Charlotte's stomach clenching down hard at the memory of how utterly shameless she'd been in there. Daniel hadn't had to seduce her into anything, either. She'd been more than willing to go down on her knees before him.

She would never be truly satisfied with just sex. She wanted Daniel to love her as well as make love to her. But that wasn't going to happen, so making love was the next best thing.

As she washed her hands, her reflection in the mirror mocked her private misery. She looked great. Glowing, in fact. Eyes bright. Lips pink. Glossy hair still tidy in its sleek ponytail, though it was slightly damp. She was even still wearing her earrings.

Shaking her head again at the irony of it all, she took the earrings off and left them on the vanity top before heading for the veranda. And Daniel. Her heartbeat quickened immediately, her nipples hardening against the soft cotton of the bathrobe. Already, she craved for him to make love to her again. Slowly this time.

'So you're still alive,' he said with a warm smile when she stepped out onto the veranda. 'I was just about to come in and check. Come on. Sit down. I'll get you a glass of wine, and top up mine at the same time. There were a couple of bottles of white already chilled in the fridge with a welcome note on them. And a couple of bottles of red in the cupboard above.'

'They'd be the four complimentary ones that came with the holiday package,' she said as she sat down at the white wrought-iron table and leant back, trying to relax.

A laughable exercise.

'You must have been tired after your long drive

up here,' Daniel said on his return. 'Feeling better now?'

Their eyes met as he handed her the wine. 'Much,' was all she could manage.

The darkening sky suddenly lit up with a sheet of lightning, a loud clap of thunder only a second behind.

'It's going to pour down any minute,' Daniel said, and settled himself back in the chair on the other side of the table. 'I love watching rain, don't you?'

'When I get the chance,' she replied, and took a sip of the chilled wine. 'What is this, a Verdelho?'

'Spot-on. From the Hunter Valley, of course. I read the label. It's damned good. We'll have to go round some of the local vineyards tomorrow and buy some wine.'

'All right,' she agreed. She supposed they couldn't stay in this room doing nothing but make love for the next four days and nights. Though she wouldn't have minded.

'Here comes the rain,' he said excitedly as large drops began falling on the colour-bond roof.

She found herself staring at his suddenly boyish face and wondering what kind of man he might have been if his father hadn't betrayed his mother. Would he have still become the love 'em and leave 'em type? Or would he have wanted marriage and children?

At least Gary had wanted marriage and children. No doubt he was already planning to marry his PA, whereas what was *she* doing? Wasting some more of her life on a man who would never give her what she wanted.

Daniel glanced over at her.

'You're thinking,' he said, his dark eyes glittering. 'Nothing good comes of thinking too much. Why don't you come over here? Bring your wine with you.'

It was close to what she'd thought about doing, sitting on his lap, making loving small talk and sipping wine together. But not quite.

Within no time Daniel put his glass down, his right hand slipping inside the top of her robe.

'I love your breasts,' he murmured as he teased her already erect nipples into points of the most exquisite sensitivity. When he pinched one of them, some of Charlotte's wine spilt into her lap.

He took the glass from her hand and put it down before returning his attention to her burning nipples, covering her left ear with his mouth at the same time and blowing softly inside.

'Daniel,' she choked out pleadingly as she squirmed against him.

'Tell me what you want,' he replied in that low, sexy voice which thrilled her.

Daniel seemed to like talking when he made love, liked complimenting and commanding her, liked making her give voice to her desires.

'You,' she groaned.

'Out here?'

'Yes,' she answered shakily.

Within no time he'd twisted her round. The air was thick, the storm about to break in earnest.

Lightning lit up the dark sky as he entered her, his hands gripping her hips once he was safely inside and pulling her back down onto him. The breath she was holding rushed from her lungs, her moan of pleasure silenced by another crash of thunder.

'Good?' he asked huskily.

Charlotte could only nod, emotion welling up within her.

I love you, she longed to say. But did not dare. Instead, she cupped his face with her hands and kissed him. Not wildly, but slowly and sensuously. She licked his lips. Sucked on the tip of his tongue. Teased the roof of his mouth with her own tongue, all the things he'd done to her.

The sudden sound of a door banging had her head jerking up, her eyes darting nervously around.

'You…you don't think someone could walk round and see us, do you?' Their veranda was reasonably private, but overlooked the extensive grounds, with several paths winding their way through the lawns and gardens.

'Not in this storm,' he reassured her. 'Everyone will be staying safely indoors.'

The rain was coming down heavily now, beating noisily against the roof.

He cupped her face and kissed *her* this time, showing her she still had a lot to learn. She whimpered when he stopped.

'I think we can dispense with this, don't you?' he murmured, undoing the sash on her robe.

Charlotte's head spun as he slowly pushed it back

off her shoulders till it fell down her arms, leaving her totally naked.

The air, cooler now with the rain, made her shiver, goose pimples breaking out all over her skin.

'I hate wasting wine,' he said, and, picking up his glass, trickled the rest of the contents over one of her throbbing breasts. She was still gasping when he picked up her glass and doused the other breast. When he leant forward and licked at her wet nipples, her gasps swiftly turned to groans. She started rocking back and forth on him, creating even more electric sensations than what was happening with her breasts.

'Yes,' he urged when she pressed her toes down and used them to lever her body up and down. He grabbed her hips and helped her, pushing her body upwards then pulling her back down onto him.

'Yes,' he ground out. 'Yes. That's the way, my darling. Aaah…'

Was it his hotly delivered endearment which tumbled her over the edge? Or his own flesh exploding within her?

Whatever, she came with a rush, bringing her wild ride to an abrupt halt. Her spasms froze her mid-movement, her mouth falling open as her head tipped back, her lungs dragging in much-needed air.

For a few seconds she just shook. And then she started dissolving around him. Disintegrating, really. She sank back down onto his lap, her head now falling forward. His arms moved to wrap around her, holding her close. Only then did she hear his breathing, which was even more ragged than her own.

Charlotte stayed that way for a long time, with no sense of time, or place. She was just there, all soft and sated and spent.

The ringing of her cellphone dragged her back to partial reality.

She groaned. Why, oh, why did phones ring at the most inopportune time?

'Don't answer it,' Daniel muttered, his arms tightening around her.

For about thirty seconds she obeyed him, wanting to do nothing but wallow in the comforting cocoon of his body. But the phone didn't stop, forcing her further out of her dream world and evoking anxious thoughts.

Not many people had her mobile number. Work. Her parents. Louise. It wouldn't be work, she reasoned logically. Which left her parents or Louise.

Charlotte couldn't imagine her parents ringing her on the first night of her supposed honeymoon, not unless it was an emergency. She hoped and prayed they hadn't had an accident driving home today. She couldn't bear it if anything had happened to her parents.

'I have to answer it,' she said at last. If it was Louise, wanting to gossip, she was going to kill her.

'If you must,' Daniel said, pulling the robe gently up onto her shoulders then lifting her even more gently off him. Charlotte threw him a slightly embarrassed smile before wrapping the robe around herself and dashing inside.

Her still ringing phone was resting just inside her carry-all, which she'd dropped on the small writing desk in the corner. Scooping it up, she pressed the button then put the tiny pink instrument to her ear.

'Yes?' she said anxiously.

'It's me, Charlotte. Louise.'

'Louise. I think I'm going to kill you.'

'Did I interrupt something? Oh, dear, I'm so sorry. But I knew you'd want to hear my news.'

'What news?' Charlotte said wearily.

'You'll never guess.'

'Then I suggest you just tell me.'

Daniel was thoughtful as he sipped his wine and waited for Charlotte to return.

Their lovemaking since arriving here, he realised, had been different from the previous night. More intense.

In some ways, the sex was more exciting. Mind-blowing, really. But there was an air of wild desperation about Charlotte that bothered him.

Especially just now…

Daniel frowned. Just how far could he have pushed that episode? Was it *love* making her more co-operative and daring?

Daniel worried that he might not be helping his cause. He vowed to cool it a little, get back to making love more tenderly, and behind closed doors. He wanted her to learn to love him.

All his worries and resolves were momentarily forgotten when Charlotte walked back out onto the veranda, the robe now firmly sashed around her. She didn't return to his lap, but slumped down on the other chair, on the other side of the table.

'Is there anything wrong?' he asked.

'No, no, nothing wrong. That was Louise. She and Brad are engaged. She finally decided to marry him.'

'Brad will be thrilled. So why are *you* upset?'

'I'm not upset,' she denied. 'I'm very happy for them both.'

She didn't look happy. She looked sad. Daniel couldn't stand her looking sad.

She glanced over at him, her expression almost bitter. 'She said it was because of something *I* said.'

'And what was that?'

Charlotte shrugged disconsolately. 'I told her I couldn't use men as she used Brad. Apparently, it set Louise thinking. She said she realised she *did* love Brad, and that if she didn't marry him she'd really regret it. So today she told him she loved him and said yes, she would marry him. They're going out to celebrate tonight.'

'I'm pleased for them. Though they are an odd match.'

'Maybe, but Brad truly loves Louise,' she said.

Daniel began to see why this news might upset Charlotte. Her best friend was getting married, whereas she'd just been jilted. Her best friend had a man who truly loved her whereas all she'd ever had were men like Dwayne and Gary.

Till now.

He'd been going to wait a lot longer before telling her he loved her, but clearly the time had come.

'You *are* upset,' he said gently. 'It doesn't take a

genius to know why. But Charlotte, you are a beautiful, sexy girl, with a sweet and loving soul. Dwayne and Gary were both fools. Let me tell you that—'

'Don't you dare say that there's someone out there who'll truly love me one day, Daniel,' she snapped, jumping to her feet and whirling to face him. 'Don't you dare. What would you know about love, anyway? You've never been in love. You don't know what it's like to love someone and not be loved back. It…it breaks your heart. It… Oh…' she groaned, and burst into tears.

Daniel was on his feet in an instant, reaching forward in an attempt to draw her into his arms.

But she wrenched away from him, dashing the tears from her eyes as she staggered back a step.

'No, no more!' she proclaimed, clutching the robe up around her neck. 'No more tears. And no more of this. I can't bear it. It's stupid and futile. I'm going inside to get dressed,' she said feverishly. 'And then I'll be driving back to Sydney.' And she began to run inside.

Daniel dashed after her, grabbing her by the shoulders and spinning her round. Their eyes clashed, hers flashing with bitter resentment, his darkly desperate.

'I wasn't going to say that there was someone out there who would truly love you one day. I was going to say that there's someone right *here* who truly loves you right *now*!'

Charlotte stared up at him for a moment, stunned. But her shock was swiftly replaced by anger.

'I don't believe you! You're lying!'

'I have no reason to lie, Charlotte. I *love* you.'

'No,' she said, shaking her head at him. *'No!'*

Things like this didn't happen to her. Guys dumped her. Rejected her. Jilted her. *Used* her.

Daniel was just lying to get her to stay, so that he could keep on sleeping with her, which she'd been only too willing to let him do.

'I *do* love you,' he insisted. 'The only reason I didn't tell you earlier was because I was worried you wouldn't believe me. I wanted to give you time to get over Gary.'

'I was over Gary in a heartbeat,' she told him, then wished she hadn't when she saw the gleam of triumph in his eyes.

'That's because you fell in love with me,' he said, pulling her forcefully back into his arms. 'You did, didn't you? Admit it. Don't lie to me.'

'So what if I did?' she threw up at him. 'What good will it do me?'

She watched, amazed, when his head tipped back in a gesture that smacked of raw relief. 'Thank you, God.'

When his eyes returned to her they were no longer desperate, or distressed. Just very determined.

'No more nonsense, then. You love me. I love you. We'll get married for real next time.'

Charlotte's mouth dropped open. 'But you told me you were allergic to marriage!'

'You cured me.'

'How very convenient.'

'Don't be cynical. It doesn't suit you. You know I love you. You know it. In your heart.'

Maybe. But her heart had always steered her wrong. Both Dwayne and Gary had claimed to love her and they had both betrayed her. She had to listen to her head this time. 'I think you're saying what you know I want you to say.'

His face showed frustration. 'What do I have to do to convince you? I'm asking you to marry me. As soon as it can be arranged.'

'And how soon can a divorce be arranged, Daniel? I've heard you have some very speedy ones in America. You won't even have to pay for a lawyer!'

'I won't go back to America. I mean, I will temporarily. I'll have to wind things up there. But I'll come back and marry you here. We'll raise our children here.'

'Our…our children?' Her heart wobbled. He was promising her children as well?

'Of course. When true love strikes, a man changes his mind about a lot of things. I want to have children with you, my darling. I thought that was what you wanted, too.'

'I…I do. I just… Oh, Daniel, it's so hard to find trust after you've been hurt as many times as I've been hurt.'

'I know,' he said, holding her closer and stroking her hair. 'I know. Truly. But trust will come with time. You wait and see.'

She wasn't so sure. Time had often been her enemy. Would Daniel still love her when he went back to America? Were his feelings an illusion, as Gary's had been? She didn't doubt he thought he was in love with her. But male love was so often based on nothing but sex. He didn't really know her, did he?

'Tell me you love me,' he demanded. 'Go on. Tell me.'

'I love you,' she choked out with far too much feeling. Now he'd know she was crazy about him.

'And you'll marry me?'

'Please don't ask me that,' she said, pulling back far enough to look up at him. 'Not yet. It's too quick. Try to understand, Daniel. I mean, you…you might go home and change your mind and…and…'

'I won't change my mind.' His handsome face was quite serious, his eyes strong.

'I can't think straight when I'm in your arms.'

'Good.' He kissed her then, a long, seductive kiss that left her reeling.

'Now I'm asking you again,' he murmured against her mouth. 'Will you marry me?'

Charlotte stiffened her spine, and her resolve. 'I told you. *No*,' she repeated, feeling quite proud of herself. 'Not yet.'

'How long do I have to wait?'

'I don't know.'

'For pity's sake, Charlotte, I thought you were dying to get married and have kids. You're not getting any younger, you know, and neither am I!'

Charlotte could appreciate the logic in this, but she was past acting like some desperate. She'd been there, done that, and she wasn't going along that road again. It was clear men didn't respect women who fell in with their plans too easily. She wanted Daniel's respect as much as she wanted his love.

'I'm not going to be bullied into saying yes just because I love you. Marriage is a very big step for two people who've only known each other for a few days. Ask me again in a month.'

'A month! I'll probably be back in LA in a month!'

Charlotte refused to be swayed. 'You can ask me when you return to Sydney, then,' she said. 'I refuse to be proposed to by email, or by phone. I will want to see you face to face. With a ring in your hand.'

He looked totally exasperated for a few seconds. But then the clouds cleared from his face and he smiled. 'Fair enough. I can wait that long, provided we spend every minute of every day I have left here in Australia with each other.'

'I have to go back to work next week.'

He sighed. 'OK. Every minute of every day *this* week. And every minute of every night *next* week,' he amended. 'Is that a deal?'

'I suppose so.' See, Charlotte? It sounds as if all he's interested in is sex.

'Another thing. When I get back from LA I think we should start trying for a baby.'

'What? You *want* me to get pregnant?'

'The sooner the better. Then you'll know I'm serious.'

'But I can't have a baby without being married!' she protested. 'Mum and Dad will have a pink fit.'

'Have you forgotten? They think we're already married. We were married yesterday.'

'But we weren't. Not really.'

'*We* know that,' he said, 'but *they* don't know that.

My plan is that we'll get married quietly as soon as possible after you say yes. Hopefully, you'll say yes before you become pregnant. I'd like to think you're not just marrying me because I'm the father of your child. Of course, that does leave your folks thinking your name is Mrs Cantrell, which is something I couldn't stand. So then we tell your parents the truth. But they love you, and they seemed to love me when they met me. They'll accept it.'

Charlotte had to laugh. Because they probably would. 'You're arrogant and ruthless when you want something, aren't you?'

'No. I'm ruthless when I love someone. And I love you, Charlotte Gale.'

Charlotte couldn't help thrilling to his declaration. But she needed more convincing.

'What is it that you love about me?'

'I love it that you would ask such a question,' he said, and scooped her up into his arms.

Charlotte tried to keep her head as he carried her inside and lowered her down onto the bed. 'That's no answer,' she said, sounding far too breathless.

'Nothing I say at this moment would satisfy you, my darling,' he said as he began undressing her. 'Let me concentrate on the one area where I can.'

'You won't change my mind with sex, you know.'

His smile carried far too much confidence for her liking. 'Probably not,' he murmured, his lips busily making their way down her already tense body. 'But a man can try, can't he?'

CHAPTER NINETEEN

'THAT'S my boarding call,' Daniel said.

'Yes, I heard it,' Charlotte replied, struggling for composure. The moment she'd been dreading had finally arrived.

The past two weeks had gone far too quickly. The days up at the Hunter Valley had been incredible. Like a real honeymoon. They'd only left the room for breakfast and the occasional swim. Dinner was always ordered from Room Service. They hadn't made it round to the wineries till the morning they checked out.

The ten days since their return to Sydney had been just as wonderful, despite Charlotte having to return to work. Somehow, being away from Daniel during the day made the time spent with him each evening all the sweeter. He'd taken her home to his sister's place for dinner a couple of evenings. And they'd gone out with Brad and Louise, once to the movies and another time to a club. But most evenings they'd spent alone, making love and talking endlessly, with Daniel really opening up to her about his life.

She'd been startled to learn just how rich he was, but not at all unhappy. How could she be unhappy about his having the means to throw up his job in America and come back to her?

That was his plan, to be back with her as soon as possible.

Charlotte had been happy with this plan, in principle, but now that the moment was here she felt nothing but dismay. And panic. What if he never came back?

'I don't have to get on that plane, Charlotte,' he said, his eyes searching hers. 'Just give me the nod and I'll cancel my flight.'

Charlotte swallowed. How easy it would be to just say yes. Cancel it. Stay with me. But he had to go back some time, logic told her. It might as well be today. He'd already delayed his flight till the Sunday so that she didn't have to take a day off work to see him off. Any further delay would make his going all the harder.

She was grateful, however, that Brad and Louise were able to be here with her. Without them, she might have broken down and begged him to stay. This way, she had to keep herself together. Louise still didn't seem convinced that Daniel was the real deal. Brad was the only one to totally approve of their whirlwind romance. Oh, and Daniel's sister, Beth. She seemed to be all for them both, which was some comfort.

Charlotte shook her head.

'You're not going to cry, are you?' Daniel asked, squeezing her hand, the one that was now bare of all rings. She'd finally mailed Gary's ring back to him, and put the wedding ring in a drawer.

'No, no. I'll be fine,' she choked out. 'Just promise

to call me as soon as you arrive. It doesn't matter what time it is here.'

'I don't think she should stay and watch the plane go,' Daniel advised Louise and Brad. 'I think you should take her away right now. Go on. Off you go.'

'Aren't you going to kiss me goodbye?' she asked plaintively.

'I'm much better at kissing hello,' he said. 'So no, I'm not going to kiss you goodbye, because this isn't goodbye. Just *au revoir*. Brad,' he said, giving Brad a sharp nod in the direction of the exits.

'Right, mate. Come on, Charlotte. Time to go.'

Charlotte threw Louise an anguished look. But she wasn't getting too much sympathy there. Louise took her arm on one side, with Brad on the other. One last desperate glance over her shoulder caught a glimpse of Daniel heading for the boarding gate. But then she lost sight of him as a group of people moved to block her view.

He was gone.

She didn't get very far before her chin began to quiver.

Her suddenly jelly-like legs only carried her a few more steps before she burst into tears. Walking farther was out of the question. She just wanted to sink to the ground right where she was and cry and cry.

'I knew something like this was going to happen,' Louise muttered as she dragged her distraught friend over to a nearby row of seats. Charlotte collapsed into one of them, her head dropping into her hands, her shoulders shaking.

'There, there, honey,' Louise said as she patted

Charlotte's back. 'You'll be fine once he calls. He's not gone for good. I'm sure he loves you. I've just been a silly, cynical cow thinking otherwise.'

'No, *I'm* the silly, cynical cow!' Charlotte burst out, her tear-stained face jerking up. 'He told me he loved me. He asked me to marry him. And all I could say was not yet. I miss him so much already. I'd give anything in the world to go back in time and tell him that I don't want him to go. Oh, Louise, what have I done?'

New tears welled up and her head dropped back into her hands. So she didn't see Daniel walk slowly towards her.

Louise did, however, her mouth dropping open.

Daniel put his fingers to his lips in a shushing gesture. Louise's eyes swung to Brad, who was grinning.

Thank goodness, she thought as she quietly stood up and gave her seat to Daniel, who sat and slid his arm across Charlotte's still trembling shoulders.

'You promised not to cry,' he said softly.

Charlotte's head whipped up, her sodden eyes flinging wide with shock and joy. 'Daniel!' she cried. 'You came back.'

He smiled. 'My shortest plane flight ever. I didn't even get to my seat.'

Daniel reached to wipe the tears from her cheeks. 'I just couldn't bear to leave you, my darling.'

'Oh, Daniel!'

'When I do go—and I will have to at some time to tie things up in the States—would you quit your job and come with me?'

'In a heartbeat.'

'And if I asked you again right now to marry me, what would you say?'

She smiled through her tears. 'You really have to ask me that?'

'Yes, I do.' And he drew a ring box out of his pocket and flipped it open. 'I want to put this on your finger before you change your mind.'

Charlotte stared down at the huge diamond solitaire and tried not to cry.

'I bought it one day whilst you were at work,' he added. 'I wanted to always have it at the ready, if and when the opportunity came to ask you again. I hope you like it.'

'I love it. But…but I want us to tell my parents as soon as possible.'

'Charlotte, I'll drive up with you and we'll explain everything together. I'm sure your mum and dad will understand. All they ever wanted was for their darling little girl to be happy. And you are happy, aren't you?'

Her eyes flooded anew with happiness.

He smiled, and slipped the ring on her finger.

It was a perfect fit. Just as they were.

Daniel sighed a truly happy sigh of his own. 'Now I think it's time for that hello kiss.'

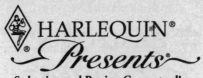

HARLEQUIN® *Presents*

Seduction and Passion Guaranteed!

Legally wed, but he's never said…
"I love you."

They're…

Wedlocked!

**The series
where
marriages are
made in haste…
and love
comes later…**

**Look out for more Wedlocked! marriage stories
in Harlequin Presents throughout 2005.**

**Coming in April:
THE BILLION-DOLLAR BRIDE**
by Kay Thorpe
#2462

**Coming in May:
THE DISOBEDIENT BRIDE**
by Helen Bianchin
#2463

**Coming in June:
THE MORETTI MARRIAGE**
by Catherine Spencer
#2474

www.eHarlequin.com

HPWL2

Seduction and Passion Guaranteed!

POSSESSED BY THE SHEIKH

An enthralling story set in the desert kingdom of Zuran

After being left stranded in the desert, Katrina was rescued by a robed man on a horse and taken back to his luxury camp. Despite the attraction that sparked between them, the sheikh thought Katrina nothing more than a whore. But there was no way he could leave her to other men. He would have to marry her. And then he discovered—firsthand—that she was a virgin....

On sale April, #2457

Arabian Nights

If you enjoyed what you just read,
then we've got an offer you can't resist!

Take 2 bestselling love stories FREE!

Plus get a FREE surprise gift!

HARLEQUIN®

Presents

Seduction and Passion Guaranteed!

The
O'CONNELLS

by

Sandra Marton

In order to marry,
they've got to gamble on love!

Welcome to the world of the wealthy Las Vegas family
the O'Connells. Take Keir, Sean, Cullen, Fallon, Megan
and Briana into your heart as they begin that most
important of life's journeys—a search for deep,
passionate, all-enduring love.

Coming in Harlequin Presents®
April 2005 #2458

Briana's story:

THE SICILIAN MARRIAGE
by *Sandra Marton*

Gianni Firelli is used to women trying to get into his bed.
So when Briana O'Connell purposely avoids him, she
instantly catches his interest. Briana most definitely
does not want to be swept off her feet by any man.
Or so she thinks, until she meets Gianni....

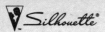

INTIMATE MOMENTS™

Explosive action,
explosive passion
from

CINDY DEES!

Charlie Squad

*No mission is too dangerous for these
modern-day warriors when lives—
and love—are on the line.*

She was his enemy's daughter. But Julia Ferrare had
called *him*—soldier Jim "Dutch" Dutcher—for help
in escaping from her father. She was beautiful,
fragile, kind…and most likely setting him up for
a con. Ten years ago, she'd stolen his family, his
memories, his heart. He'd be a fool to trust her
again. But sometimes even a hardened soldier
could be a fool…for love.

Her Secret Agent Man
by Cindy Dees

Silhouette Intimate Moments #1353

On sale March 2005!

Only from Silhouette Books!

Visit Silhouette Books at www.eHarlequin.com   SIMHSAM1

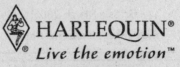